Creature of Magic

Far ahead, by the reeds where she'd first met Kelvin, Molly caught sight of something black moving through the water. Her eyes widened and she came to a stop as she realized it was a horse. Its magnificent black coat glistened in the sun. It tossed its head, and a rainbow of water sprayed from its heavy mane. Then it trotted into the reeds.

A moment later, the reeds parted and Kelvin emerged. There was no sign of the black horse.

Molly drew in a shuddering breath, torn between horror and absolute delight. Now she understood what Kelvin was. Now his wildness all made perfect, crazy sense.

"Oh, my gosh," she whispered. "He's a kelpie!"

The Spell of the Black Stone

WELCOME INN

#4 The Spell of the Black Stone

by E. L. FLOOD

Rainbow Bridge

Troll Associates

LIBRARY OF CONGRESS CATALOGING-IN-PUBLICATION DATA

Flood, E. L.
   The spell of the black stone / by E. L. Flood.
     p.   cm. — (Welcome Inn; #4)
   Summary: The arrival of a magic charm from Scotland for Molly's
twelfth birthday coincides with the appearance of a mischievous and
mysterious Scottish boy, who may be a water spirit called a kelpie.
   ISBN 0-8167-3430-5 (pbk.)
   [1. Supernatural—Fiction.]   I. Title.   II. Series: Flood, E. L.
Welcome Inn; #4.
PZ7.F6616Sp   1995
[Fic]—dc20   94-22760

Published by Troll Associates, Inc. Rainbow Bridge is a trademark of Troll Associates.

Printed in the United States of America.

10 9 8 7 6 5 4 3 2 1

For Seth

CHAPTER ONE

"How could Josh do this to me?" Molly O'Brien muttered to herself. "How could Ms. Groening do this to me? How could any of them do it? I thought they *liked* me!"

Molly shifted the straps of her knapsack on her shoulders, making a face as the nylon brushed against her sticky bare arms. It was Monday, just after school. She was walking home to Welcome Inn, the guest house run by her parents. And she was feeling sorry for herself.

It wasn't just that it was already ninety degrees and humid, even though it was only the beginning of June. No, that was bad, but what was even worse was that Molly's favorite teacher, Ms. Groening, had teamed her up with Charlotte Anderson for the

9

class's week-long science project studying wetlands ecology. They were to start tomorrow, with a field trip to DeKater Hollow.

"Sheesh, O'Brien, I'm sorry, but it isn't my fault," Molly's friend Josh Goldberg had said when she complained to him. He pushed unruly brownish-blond hair out of his eyes. "Ms. Groening is the one who decided the teams."

"Yeah, but everyone else gets to work with someone they like," Molly wailed. "You get to work with Paul Roman. How come I get stuck with *her*?"

Charlotte was Molly's worst nightmare. Except for the fact that Molly was good friends with Josh, whom Charlotte had a huge crush on, Molly couldn't think of anything she'd ever *done* to Charlotte. But for some reason, Charlotte just didn't like her.

When Molly first came to Blackberry Island Middle School, Charlotte had done her best to make the new kid feel like a complete jerk. She never lost an opportunity to make fun of Molly's clothes, or the way she wore her hair, or even the fact that she was a year younger than the rest of the seventh-graders.

After Molly started making friends, Charlotte backed off a little. But you could still count on her for a mean comment every time Molly wore mismatched socks by accident, or got an answer wrong in class, or did anything at all that was less than perfect.

And now they were going to be stuck working together for a whole, horrible week!

As she trudged up the steep driveway to Welcome Inn, a drop of sweat ran off the tip of her nose. She brushed damp bangs off her face and gazed at the sky. Ominous blue-gray clouds were massing on the eastern horizon, out over the ocean. It was thunderstorm weather.

"Molly!" Her younger sister, Gwen, stood on the long, shady porch, waving. "Hurry up! You got a package from Uncle Jack," Gwen held up a rectangular package wrapped in brown paper as Molly ran up the porch steps. "I bet it's your twelfth birthday present."

Molly wished she hadn't run. The soupy air made breathing difficult. "Kind of late, isn't it? My birthday was last week," she said ungratefully.

Immediately, she felt guilty. Jack O'Brien, their father's brother, was an archaeologist. He tended to spend most of his time in remote places where you never knew exactly how long the mail would take. But even if his packages were often late, he had never yet failed to send Molly something really neat for her birthday.

She took the package from Gwen. "Aren't you going to open it?" Gwen pressed, her blue eyes bright with curiosity.

"In a minute," Molly said. She was studying the postmark to see where the package had been mailed. But all she could see was a P. The red ink was too smudged and water-marked to read.

In fact, the whole package looked rather tattered. The brown paper was wrinkled and blotched, and most of the stamps seemed to have peeled off. "This must have come by boat," Molly commented. "It looks like it got soaked."

Crack! At her words, a brilliant flash lit the sky, accompanied by a tremendous boom. Molly and Gwen both jumped.

"Look," Gwen gasped, pointing out to sea.

Molly caught her breath as a jagged fork of lightning lanced down from sky to water. Thunder boomed again. The sun was gone now, smothered in black clouds, and a strong wind was starting up.

"We better go in," she said. "Or *we'll* be the ones who get soaked."

As they came into the front hall, their older brother, Andrew, hurried by. "I'm closing all the windows on the first floor," he said. "You two get the rest of the house."

"Right." Setting her package on the hall table, Molly sped up the two flights of steps to her room, which was on the third floor at the base of a small, round tower.

When she'd closed her own window, she ran back down to the second floor to help Gwen.

"Get Room One," Gwen called over her shoulder. "I got everything else."

The four second-floor guest rooms were grouped together in a hall that ran the length of the front of the house. Molly flung open the door to Room One.

The windows were wide open and wind was sweeping in. A vase of dried wildflowers had blown off the desk and shattered on the floor. Molly closed the windows, then grabbed a dustpan and brush to clean up the mess.

Creak! The old building groaned under the wind's pummeling fist. Gazing anxiously out the window, Molly wondered if they'd be all right. The inn was so exposed, alone on a hilltop with only a few scraggly bushes to protect it.

Before her eyes, the sky grew darker and darker. Though it wasn't even five yet, it looked like night outside. And then, with a clatter like a million pebbles, the rain struck.

Without thinking, Molly jumped backward as a wall of water hit the tall window. In an instant, it was as if she were standing behind a waterfall. The old, wavy glass shimmered with rivers of rain. Lightning flashed almost continuously, searing her eyes with weird, colorful afterimages. And over it all, the thunder crashed and boomed.

Shivering, Molly hurried out.

The front door opened just as she got downstairs, and Molly's mother and grandfather blew in along with a quantity of wind and water.

"Wheee-oh!" Grandpa Lloyd exclaimed, his blue eyes dancing. "This one's a real humdinger. That wind must be gusting fifty miles an hour! The last

June storm I remember as fierce as this was back in '72."

Mrs. O'Brien ran a hand through her cap of reddish-brown hair. "I got soaked just running from the truck to the front door. Thanks for picking me up at the ferry, Dad. I was planning to walk home. I'd probably be drowned by now!"

"Everything's under control here," Molly reported. "We closed all the windows."

Mrs. O'Brien put her arm around Molly's shoulders and gave her a brief hug. "I knew I could count on my troops. Let me go change out of my lawyer clothes, and then we'll see about getting some dinner together."

"About dinner . . ." David O'Brien, Molly's father, came through the dining room doorway. He was a tall, thin-faced man with thick, straight dark hair and dreamy brown eyes. Molly and Andrew looked just like him. Gwen did, too, except for her blazing blue eyes. Those came from Grandpa Lloyd and Mrs. O'Brien.

"What about dinner?" Mrs. O'Brien said, a worried look coming over her face.

"We've had three reservations canceled already," Mr. O'Brien said. "The forecasters have put out a severe-storm warning until at least nine o'clock tonight."

"Weathermen," Grandpa Lloyd grumbled. "Count on 'em being one hundred percent wrong."

Mrs. O'Brien raised her eyebrows at her husband. "How many other tables do we have booked for tonight?"

"Just one, the Seymours," Mr. O'Brien said.

Faintly over the shriek of the wind, they heard the office phone ring. A second later Andrew yelled from the study, "The Seymours canceled their reservation!"

Mrs. O'Brien frowned. "This isn't good."

Molly bit her lip. She knew her mother was worried about business. When they'd first moved to Blackberry Island, the inn had been run-down, with a bad reputation from its previous owner. They'd all worked hard to fix it up, and the combination of the pleasant rooms and Mr. O'Brien's delicious cooking had finally started to attract customers.

But now that the summer season had started and they should be overflowing with customers, it seemed there was one problem after another. Recently a leak in the hot-water pipes had forced them to cancel all their room reservations for a week while they had the upstairs plumbing redone. And now the storm was making them lose their dinner customers.

"Most of the food will keep till tomorrow," Mr. O'Brien said. "But I've got to cook those crabs tonight. Guess we're going to have a feast."

"All right!" Molly yelled. She was sorry that the inn was losing business, but steamed crab was one of her all-time favorite foods.

It was a gloriously messy meal, eaten around the

big kitchen table, which had been spread with newspapers. Molly, dipping her sixth crab claw into the bowl of drawn butter and, listening to the wind and rain lash the house, felt so good that she almost stopped worrying about Charlotte and the science project. Almost.

It wasn't till the whole family was sitting in the front parlor later that night that Molly remembered the package from Uncle Jack. Hurrying out to the hall table, she grabbed it and brought it in.

"Pennyahael," her father pronounced when she showed him the strange postmark. "It's a town on the Isle of Mull, in Scotland. Jack's there visiting one of his old professors."

Molly unwrapped the brown paper eagerly. Inside were two books. *Celtic Legends* was the title of the one on top. The other was called *Myths and Folktales from the Scottish Islands.*

"Books? Is that all?" Gwen's voice was disappointed.

Though she didn't say anything, Molly was disappointed, too. She loved to read, and she liked myths and legends a lot, but usually Uncle Jack's presents were a little more—well, unusual.

When she tossed the brown wrapper into the metal trash can, it clanged. "Hey, stupid, there's something else in there," Andrew said.

Molly retrieved the wrapper from the can and shook it. A smooth black stone fell into her hand,

16

and a sheet of notepaper fluttered to the floor.

"It's a note from Uncle Jack," said Gwen, picking it up and handing it to Molly, who read it aloud.

Dear Molly,

Scotland seems alive with magic. Being here is like being in one of the books I've sent you. They'll tell you all about the kinds of magical creatures, or Sith (pronounced *shee*), that you might encounter here. And the stone, I'm told, will give you mastery over one of them. It's called a Sith-stone, and the man who sold it to me assures me that it's genuine. However, I did notice he had dozens of identical ones in a drawer in his shop. I suspect he does quite well selling them to gullible tourists like myself. Oh, well, the carving is interesting. If nothing else, it'll make a nice paperweight. Happy birthday.

Love,
Uncle Jack

Intrigued, Molly studied the black stone. It fit perfectly into the palm of her hand. An intricately carved pattern of twining serpents decorated its surface.

Opening *Celtic Legends*, she stopped to stare at the frontispiece. It was a painting of a magnificent black horse in the act of plunging into a turbulent river. On the horse's back was a young woman in flowing clothing, her mouth open in a scream. "The Kelpie carries Janet Beaton to a watery grave," said the caption. "Kelpies can take the form of beast or man."

"Cool," Molly said aloud. She flipped through the book, looking for more pictures.

There was one of a mermaid seated on a rock, calmly combing her long tresses, while in the background a man struggled to keep from drowning. "The treacherous mermaid ignores the sailor's cries for help. Mermaids lure men to their deaths by singing," said that caption.

"Creepy," murmured Gwen, who was looking over Molly's shoulder.

Molly shot her an annoyed glance and moved to the love seat. Curling her feet under her, she opened to the beginning of the book and began to read about the Selkie, whatever that was. As she read, she rubbed her thumb absently over the back of the Sith-stone. It had a funny texture, so smooth and friction-less that it felt wet, though Molly knew it wasn't.

Outside, the wind's shrieking climbed to a higher pitch. Mrs. O'Brien got up and moved to the window. "This storm is really something," she said, sounding worried.

Fzzt! A bolt of lightning temporarily made the parlor as bright as day. At the same instant, thunder cracked right overhead.

A split second later, the lights went out and the room was plunged into darkness.

CHAPTER TWO

The dark was absolute, inky. Gwen let out a scream and threw her arms around Molly's neck.

"Let go. You're choking me!" Molly said.

"Everyone be calm," came Mr. O'Brien's voice. "We blew a fuse, that's all."

"Blew all of them is more like it," Grandpa Lloyd commented. "Andrew, what say you and I go down to the basement and see what we can do?"

He didn't bother to ask Mr. O'Brien. The kids all knew their father was a terrible klutz when it came to anything mechanical.

"There are some candles in the dining room," Mrs. O'Brien said. "I'll get them."

Molly heard her mother groping across the room. There was a thud and a muffled curse. Mrs. O'Brien had hit the wing chair near the door, Molly guessed. Then came the sound of the parlor door opening and closing.

A few moments later, Mrs. O'Brien came back, preceded by stars of mellow light from the branching candelabrum she held. Andrew and Grandpa Lloyd came into the room right behind her. Andrew had a heavy flashlight in his hand.

Grandpa Lloyd shook his head in response to Mrs. O'Brien's questioning expression. "They're all out, just as I thought," he said. "Every single fuse is blown. And you people don't have any spares!"

Mr. O'Brien seemed embarrassed. "I've been meaning to pick some up," he murmured.

"Well . . ." Mrs. O'Brien sighed. "Gwen, Molly, go around the house and collect all the candlesticks you can find. I guess we're going to have a real old-fashioned evening."

The next morning Molly overslept because her electric alarm clock wasn't working. "I might as well stay home," she said hopefully to her father at breakfast. "My class has probably already left for the field trip to DeKater Hollow."

"That's all right," he said. "I'll drop you off there. I've got to drive into town and buy some fuses anyway."

Rats! It looked as if there would be no way to escape Charlotte. Molly's face was glum as she swallowed the last of her orange juice.

As the car bumped along Gravers Lane, though, Molly's spirits began to rise. The storm of the night before had washed away the heat and humidity, and now the sun bathed everything in a warm, gentle radiance. The young leaves on the trees shimmered as if new made, and every blade of grass cast a clean, dark shadow. The knot in Molly's stomach eased a little.

That is, until they pulled up by the small school bus where her class was milling around, and she climbed out of the car and faced Charlotte's cold blue eyes and heard her purposely loud whisper. "Look!" Charlotte said. "The baby brain's *daddy* brought her. Nice outfit," she added, staring at Molly's old gym shorts and faded T-shirt. A couple of the girls standing with Charlotte snickered.

Molly's cheeks turned crimson. She had purposely worn old clothes because Ms. Groening had told them they'd be splashing around in the mud and getting dirty. But leave it to Charlotte, immaculate in white shorts and a pale blue polo shirt, to make her feel like a complete slob.

Molly's friend Ann Chiu, who was also part of Charlotte's crowd, gave her a sympathetic look but said nothing. Molly turned away, feeling a sudden spurt of anger. Why doesn't Ann ever stand up to Charlotte? she wondered. If it were my friend who was being put down and teased all the time, I'd have something to say about it!

Ms. Groening clapped her hands. She was a small, energetic woman with lots of curly brown hair and thoughtful gray eyes. Molly liked her a lot. "Okay, class, listen up," she called.

The twenty or so seventh-graders gathered into a ragged circle around Ms. Groening. Across the circle, Molly spotted Josh with his partner, Paul Roman. He grinned, his green eyes crinkling at the corners, and gave her the thumbs-up, but she just scowled back. It was going to be a terrible morning, she could tell.

"Today we're going to look at the elements that make up the ecosystem of a wetland," Ms. Groening said. She waved a hand at the small, marshy lake in the bottom of the hollow. "Let's start by making a list of the animals you might expect to find right here in DeKater Hollow."

"Fish," someone yelled.

"Ducks," said someone else.

"Herons," Molly added. She was thinking of the other time she'd been to DeKater Hollow, early that spring. She'd been in the middle of an exciting adventure that time, but she would never forget her sense of wonder at the sight of a tall blue heron standing motionless among the reeds.

Other people suggested frogs, snakes, turtles, squirrels, insects, and all kinds of other animals. Ms. Groening had each two-person team make a list of things to look for.

"And what about plants?" Ms. Groening said.

"Trees."

"Water lilies."

"Algae," Molly suggested.

"Algae isn't a plant. It's just green slime," Charlotte said.

"Actually, Molly's right," Ms. Groening said, smiling at Molly. "Algae *is* a plant. And it's a very important part of a wetlands ecosystem."

Charlotte slid Molly a contemptuous glance. "Teacher's pet," she muttered.

Molly flushed, wishing she had kept her mouth shut.

The class went on listing plants until Ms. Groening thought they had enough to start with. Then she gave a magnifier and several plastic bags to each team. "Now we start observing," she said. "Go around the hollow and see what you can find. If you spot one of the plants or animals from our list, check it off. If you spot something that isn't on the list, add it. If you spot something you don't recognize, make a guess at what it is or make up a name for it. Then write a complete description. One person can describe while the other records. If it's a bird, how big is it? What color are its feathers? Does it swim? Is it part of a flock? If it's a plant, how tall is it? What shape are the leaves? What do they look like under the magnifier? Draw pictures if you like. Each team ought to be able to find at least five kinds of plants and five animals."

Josh raised his hand. "Can we take samples?"

"Good question," Ms. Groening said. "You may collect leaves and small pieces of bark from plants—that's what the plastic bags are for—but please don't be greedy. And no collecting frogs, snakes, insects, or any other animals. We can study them perfectly well without frightening or hurting them.

"Any questions? Okay, get going!"

The group broke up and the teams began to spread out over the hollow. Charlotte, ignoring Molly, was making for the water's edge. Sighing, Molly followed her.

It could have been a great day, she thought. They were outside, with the sun shining and a gentle breeze blowing. And they were going to spend the next couple of hours just looking at plants and animals. If Josh had been her partner, the science project would have been downright *fun*!

But she was stuck with Charlotte. Well, she might as well try to make the best of it.

"Where are we going?" she asked, catching up to the taller girl as they walked past a small, sandy strip where a couple of canoes and a rowboat were beached.

Charlotte didn't answer, just looked annoyed and pointed to the far shore of the lake.

"What's over there?" Molly persisted. "Is there some special plant or something?"

Charlotte gave her a withering stare. "I'm not looking for any dumb plant," she said. "I just want to get out of sight of Ms. Groaning."

24

Molly pressed her lips together. She wasn't about to let herself in for more sneering by correcting Charlotte. In spite of its funny spelling, the teacher's name was pronounced *grayning*, and Charlotte knew that perfectly well. She was just being mean.

So instead Molly merely said, "We better look around some, at least while she can still see us. Otherwise she'll think we're goofing off."

"Fine." Stopping, Charlotte looked down at her white shorts. "*You* can collect the algae samples. I'm not doing anything that's going to make me get dirty."

"We don't have to go into the water," Molly pointed out. "We can look at stuff that grows by the water's edge, too." She knelt by a clump of delicate lavender wildflowers. "Like these. I've never seen them before. I wonder what they are?"

Charlotte squinted. "Those dinky little things? This is so *boring*."

Molly took a deep breath. She was starting to get annoyed. "Look, how about if you describe them and I'll write down what you say?" Maybe Charlotte wouldn't be such a pain if Molly did most of the work. It was worth a try, anyway.

Pulling out her notebook and pen, she took a seat on a rounded boulder. "Okay, go ahead."

"What do you want me to say?" Charlotte grumbled. "It's a flower. It's purple. Its leaves are green."

Molly waited for Charlotte to go on. When she said nothing more, Molly coached, "How many petals does the flower have?"

Charlotte counted. "Six."

Molly wrote that down. "How about the leaves? What shape are they?"

"What do you mean, what shape? They're leaf-shaped," Charlotte said irritably. "I know! I'll take a sample."

Before Molly could stop her, she had ripped the entire clump of flowers out of the ground, roots and all. Pulling the roots off, she tossed them into the lake. Then she stuffed the delicate blooms into one of the plastic bags.

Molly's mouth opened in horror. "Charlotte, you killed it! You're not supposed to rip out an entire plant! Didn't you hear what Ms. Groening said?"

Charlotte's face turned red. "'Didn't you hear what Ms. Groening said?'" she mimicked. "I don't care what Ms. Groening said. You're such a goody-goody. No wonder nobody likes you!"

At the beginning of the year, Charlotte's words would probably have made Molly cry. But by now, when she knew she had friends—good friends, like Josh, or even Ann—they just made her mad.

But not mad enough to start a fight. Molly wished she had the nerve to tell Charlotte off, or even to punch her in the nose, but she didn't. So she just turned and walked away.

"Hey, where do you think you're going?" Charlotte called after her.

Molly didn't answer. I'll do this project by myself if I have to, she thought. Let Charlotte fail, if that's what she wants. I don't care.

Her long, angry strides brought her quickly around to the far shore of DeKater Lake. A stream fed into the lake here, creating a marshy area of little islets haired with reeds taller than Molly's head and divided by slender ribbons of water.

Molly pushed through the reeds. By now her temper was beginning to cool. I might find a frog in here, she reflected. Or a turtle. Or even—

The thought broke off as she stumbled over something. Regaining her balance, she looked down to see what had tripped her.

It was a tall, black leather boot, like the kind you wear for horseback riding. Molly's brows drew together in puzzlement.

Then they shot up and her eyes widened as she saw that the boot was attached to a trousered leg. And the leg was attached to a body.

Stretched on his side among the reeds was a dark-haired boy of fourteen or fifteen. He wore a red vest over an old-fashioned white shirt with frilly cuffs. His face was pale, his eyes closed. And he lay absolutely still, as if he were dead.

CHAPTER THREE

Molly's hand flew to her mouth and she made a small, strangled sound.

The dark-haired boy opened his eyes, which were an extraordinary, rich brown, and smiled slowly at her. "Hello," he said.

"Oh!" Molly gasped. Her knees felt wobbly with relief. "I thought you were . . ."

His smile broadened. "No, just resting," he said, and sat up. He had a funny accent, she noticed, with very round O's and rolling R's. "It was a hard journey, but here I am."

"What do you mean?" Molly asked, puzzled.

The boy gazed at her for a moment. Then he laughed. "Nothing," he said. "My name is Kelvin."

"I'm Molly." She was about to ask him what he

was doing sleeping in the middle of a swamp, but Kelvin's gaze had moved beyond her. "Who's your friend?" he inquired.

Molly looked over her shoulder and suppressed a groan. Charlotte had followed her! And now she was staring at Kelvin with a very interested look in her eyes.

"I'm Charlotte Anderson," she said, still staring. "Are you a tourist here?"

Kelvin laughed. "I suppose I am. I was having a wee sleep, as you can see."

"You have the *greatest* accent," Charlotte said. "What kind is it? English? Hey, I know. You're with that group of English kids who are camping in Chapin Bay, aren't you? I talked to one of your friends yesterday. He was from Ireland, actually. I bet you're Irish, too, right?"

"Close. I'm Scots," Kelvin told her.

"Scots? You mean Scottish?" Charlotte giggled. "That's a funny way to say it. Like 'Mary, Queen of Scots.' It's kind of old-fashioned and romantic, I guess." She pointed at his frilly shirt. "I love your shirt!"

"Thank you," Kelvin said politely. Then he shot a glance full of laughter at Molly.

Molly had been getting more and more annoyed with Charlotte. It wasn't fair, the way she had come flouncing up and taken over the conversation. After all, Molly was the one who had found Kelvin, and she couldn't even get one word in edgewise! And why on earth was Charlotte speaking in that weird, breathy kind of voice? Molly suspected she was trying to sound older than she really was.

But when Kelvin gave Molly that look, she felt better. Obviously, Kelvin had seen right away what a faker Charlotte really was. He was just playing along with her to be polite.

"Are you really from Scotland?" Molly asked, seating herself on a hummock opposite him. "My uncle is there right now, visiting someone on the Isle of Mull."

"Is that so?" Kelvin looked interested. "Mull's a grand, wild place."

"I've been to Scotland. We went on a trip to the British Isles last year," Charlotte butted in. "We went to Loch Ness, but I never saw the Loch Ness Monster. Have you ever been to Loch Ness?"

"No, I've not been there, but I do have a distant relative in those parts," Kelvin told her. Again he gave Molly that warm, conspiratorial smile. Molly smiled back.

Charlotte's face darkened as she noticed this exchange. She was still standing, Molly guessed because she was worried about getting her white shorts dirty. Suddenly she leaned over and plucked a damp, green strand of some kind of water weed out of Kelvin's hair. "Ugh, what's this?" she said. "Gross! You have all kinds of plants and stuff in your hair."

"Charlotte!" Molly burned with shame. She hoped Kelvin wouldn't think that *everyone* on Blackberry Island was so rude. "He was sleeping here. Of course he has stuff in his hair."

But Kelvin didn't seem offended. "I'm not very tidy, am I?" he said cheerfully. This time his incredible smile was directed at Charlotte.

Her eyes flashed with triumph. "Here," she said, handing Molly the damp piece of weed. "Keep it as a sample, since you're the one who's so excited about the stupid science project." Then she stepped in front of Molly and actually sat down between her and Kelvin, with her back squarely to Molly. She flipped her chestnut hair over her shoulder. "Do you like cookouts?" she asked him. "My family is having a cookout tonight."

Molly was flabbergasted at Charlotte's rudeness. She was still trying to think of something devastating to say when she heard several voices coming their way.

One was Ms. Groening's. "Kids, over here," she was calling. "Ann, Becky, I bet there are all kinds of plants and animals in this marshy area."

Molly jumped to her feet. What would Ms. Groening think if she saw the two girls sitting there, talking to an older boy like Kelvin?

Surprisingly, Charlotte seemed to have had the same thought. "Come on, let's go," she said to Molly. "Otherwise Ms. Groaning will bring the whole world in here and bother Kelvin."

Kelvin didn't stir, merely giving them a little wave. But as they were turning away, he murmured, "I'll be here later." He said it so softly that Molly wasn't even sure she'd heard him right.

"What did you say?" Charlotte demanded.

He looked at her. "I said, see you later," he told her in a louder voice.

A dreamy expression settled on Charlotte's face. "Okay," she said happily.

As she turned away, Kelvin caught Molly's eye and gave her that laughing look again. And suddenly she was sure she *had* heard him correctly the first time.

"He's gorgeous," Charlotte whispered as they walked away. "And I think he likes me!"

"Right," Molly muttered.

When they came out of the reeds, they spotted Ms. Groening with Ann Chiu and Ann's partner, Becky Sheldon. Molly expected Charlotte to rush up to Ann immediately and tell her all about Kelvin, but instead Charlotte said: "There's nothing in there but a whole bunch of blackflies. You guys will get bitten to death if you go in there."

"Ugh." Ann made a face.

Ms. Groening raised her eyebrows at Molly. "Is it that bad?"

"Uh—" Molly hated to lie to Ms. Groening, and she also hated to agree with Charlotte about anything. But on the other hand, she just had a feeling it would be a bad idea—though she wasn't sure *why*—for Ms. Groening to meet Kelvin.

"We didn't see any interesting plants or animals," she said at last. That was true—if you didn't count Kelvin as an interesting animal!

"Ms. Groening!" Josh yelled from farther down the shore. "Paul and I found some turtles!"

"Great!" Ms. Groening said. She beckoned to the girls. "Let's go see what the guys have."

For the rest of the trip, Charlotte was strangely quiet. Every so often, when Molly sneaked a glance at her, she had that dumb, dreamy look on her face. Molly decided it was probably a good thing. Charlotte was no more useful as a project partner than she had been before, but at least she wasn't actively torturing her anymore.

It wasn't until the class broke for lunch that Molly was finally able to talk to Josh in private. She beckoned him behind the school bus, where they could be alone. Then, quickly, she told him about the strange boy she and Charlotte had found sleeping in the reeds, and how he had said he'd be there later.

"Weird," Josh commented. "So you think he wants to talk to you about something? But he couldn't while Charlotte was there?"

Molly nodded. "She went nuts over him the minute she saw him."

"Well, that's something, anyway," Josh said. "Maybe now she'll leave *me* alone."

"I bet she will," Molly agreed. Frowning, she added, "There's something . . . I don't know. . . *different* about this guy, Josh."

"Different how?"

"Well . . ." Molly wasn't sure how to explain. "He wears cool clothes," she said at last. "And you should see the way he smiles!"

Josh narrowed his eyes. "Are you sure you don't have a crush on him, too?"

"Josh!" Molly said, turning red. "It's not like that. That isn't what I meant at all!"

"Okay, okay, cool out," Josh said. He peeked around the end of the school bus. A noisy game of capture-the-flag had started up in the field. "We probably have about twenty minutes before we have to head back to school. Come on, let's go see the incredible Kelvin."

They slipped through the fringe of the woods until they were well away from the other kids. Then, moving fast, Molly led Josh to the reedy area where Kelvin had been lying. She forged through the reeds, waving away clouds of gnats that swarmed around her head. Funny, she hadn't noticed the bugs when she was talking to Kelvin.

But when she got to where she had left him, there was no one there. And the reeds where he had been lying weren't even bent.

"He's gone!" she said, feeling a strange wave of disappointment. "He said he'd be here."

Josh shrugged. "Maybe he meant *later* later. He probably went back to his camp for lunch."

Suddenly Molly spotted something on the muddy edge of the lake. Stepping forward, she bent down. Her brows rose in surprise. Pressed into the mud were a few big, crescent-shaped hoofprints, leading into the water.

"Hey, Josh, check this out!" she said.

"What?" Josh came up beside her and looked where she was pointing.

"Those weren't there earlier," she said. "At least, I didn't notice them."

"Maybe Kelvin had a horse," Josh suggested.

"I didn't see one."

"It could have been tied up in the woods," Josh pointed out. "Or the hoofprints could belong to someone else's horse." He checked his watch. "Look, O'Brien, it's getting late."

Molly slapped again at the cloud of gnats. "All right," she said reluctantly. "I guess we better go. But I think we should come back after school. I'm telling you, Josh, there's something about Kelvin." Looking around to make sure they were alone, she lowered her voice and added, "Something that makes me think of all kinds of adventures."

"Adventures?" Josh's green eyes grew thoughtful. "Okay, O'Brien, I'm with you. Now all we have to do is find this Kelvin."

That evening, Welcome Inn was full of diners. Molly was glad. It made it easier for her to slip away after she'd eaten her own dinner, without her parents asking where she was going.

She was headed for DeKater Hollow, where she and Josh had agreed to meet. She would have brought Gwen along, but Gwen's best friend Joanne was visiting, and she would have had to come, too. And there was no way Molly was going to let Joanne in on anything that even vaguely looked like an adventure. Joanne drove Molly crazy.

At the bottom of the driveway Molly turned left onto the main road. A little ways up on the right there was an old, overgrown lane that was part of a shortcut to DeKater Hollow. An old woman named Ernestine had shown her the shortcut.

Though it was past seven, the sun hadn't even begun to set as Molly came out in a level, grassy area with a big butternut tree in the middle. Josh was waiting for her by the tree, as they'd agreed.

"Do you really think this Kelvin guy will come back here?" Josh asked as they walked along the lake shore. "I mean, wouldn't it make more sense to look for him at his campsite?"

"He said he'd be here," Molly replied. "Hey, look! There he is!"

Ahead, near the place where she'd first seen him,

a dark-haired figure in a white shirt and red vest was wading into the lake. "Kelvin!" Molly called, waving her hand.

But he didn't seem to have heard. In the next instant he dived smoothly below the water's surface.

"Why is he swimming with his clothes on?" Josh asked.

"I don't know," Molly said. It *was* strange.

They walked toward the place where they'd seen him last. "He's sure been under a long time," Josh commented after a while.

"You're right." Molly looked for his dark head, but the lake's surface was smooth as far as she could see. A sudden knot of anxiety twisted her stomach. "Josh, do you think something's wrong?"

"You mean—could he be drowning?" Josh asked.

They stared at each other for a horrible moment. Then they both took off, running, for the water's edge.

CHAPTER FOUR

Pausing only to kick off their shoes, Molly and Josh dashed into the water. Molly gasped as icy wavelets foamed up her bare legs. Ahead of her, Josh dived in and began swimming strongly toward the spot where they'd last seen Kelvin.

Molly wasn't nearly as good a swimmer as Josh, so she bounded through knee-high water parallel to him. The lake bottom gradually sloped down, until Molly was in up to the hem of her shorts. Then she lost her footing and smacked face-first into the chilly water.

She stood up, sputtering and coughing, and flung dripping hair out of her face. Scanning the lake, she had a moment of panic as she realized that now Josh was nowhere in sight, either. Then his head broke water about twenty yards away from her. Treading water, he shouted, "I can't find him!"

"Kelvin!" Molly yelled. "Kelvin, are you all right?"

No answer.

"Josh, what are we going to do?" she cried, horror-stricken.

"Keep looking," Josh said. Then he took a deep breath and dived in again.

Grimly, Molly did the same.

Opening her eyes underwater, she found herself staring into a cloud of greenish-brown silt. She must have stirred up the lake's muddy bottom with her feet. Kicking like a frog, Molly darted away into deeper water.

Here it was even colder, and the late sun sifted through the water in long, scattered green bars. Molly swam down toward what looked like a patch of red cloth, but when she got close to it she saw it was just a piece of an old rowboat.

Her lungs were starting to hurt, so she made for the surface. Just as she broke through, the breath exploded out of her. She drew in long, gasping gulps of air and waited, treading water, until her breathing evened out again. Then she went back down.

Underneath, the silence was eerie. All Molly could hear was the threshing sound of her own arms and legs as they swept the water in a trail of little bubbles. There was no sign of Kelvin anywhere. It was hopeless, she thought. They'd never find him in time.

She came up about ten feet away from Josh.

"I couldn't . . . find him," Josh panted.

"Me, either," Molly said.

"Hello, there," came a voice from the shore. "Is the water so nice, then? Och, I'll join you myself if you don't come out soon."

Molly's head whipped around. On the shore stood a dark-haired figure in tall riding boots, with a white shirt under a red vest.

"Kelvin?" she gasped.

"Aye, who else?" he called.

"But—" In her confusion Molly forgot to tread water. "Aargh!" she gurgled, sinking in a welter of bubbles.

An instant later she felt a firm hand grasp her wrist. As she came back to the surface, coughing, Josh looped an arm around her neck and under one arm and efficiently swam with her into shallower water. "You can stand up here," he told her. "Are you okay?"

"Let me go!" Molly protested, embarrassed. "I wasn't drowning. I can swim fine!"

Josh's green eyes went wide, then darkened with anger. "I was trying to save your life," he said. "Sorry. I won't do it again."

Molly immediately felt awful. "Josh. . ." she

began. But Josh had turned away and was already sloshing toward the shore. Sighing, Molly followed.

By the time she got there, Josh was standing in front of Kelvin with his hands on his hips. "What's the big idea?" he demanded. "Do you think it's funny to pretend you're drowning so people will run in to save you and get soaked?" He slapped angrily at his wet T-shirt.

"Yeah, and why on earth were you swimming with all your clothes on?" Molly chimed in.

Kelvin stared from her to Josh. Then a smile broke over his lips. "Do I look as if I've just been swimming with all my clothes on?" he asked, gesturing with both hands at his white shirt.

Molly and Josh both looked. Molly's jaw dropped.

Kelvin's shirt was dry. What's more, it was as snowy and crisp as if it had just been starched. His red vest and his trousers were dry, too. And his boots looked freshly polished.

"How'd you change clothes so fast?" Josh asked.

"Change?" Kelvin laughed. "I've not changed. Do you think I keep a duplicate set of clothes lying about to fool people?"

When he put it that way, Molly supposed, it did sound sort of ridiculous.

Josh folded his arms. "So who was it we saw in the water, then? Your twin brother?"

Kelvin spread his hands. "Truly, how could I

know?" he said. "I've not got a twin." Cocking his head at Josh, he added with a grin, "But if I had, I'd hope you'd be on hand to rescue him, too. How did you learn to swim so well?"

Josh looked caught off guard. "Uh, I have a cousin who's a lifeguard," he mumbled. "She taught me some stuff."

"Kelvin, this is my best friend, Josh," Molly said, shivering. As the sun set, the air was starting to cool, and her wet shorts and T-shirt were making goosebumps come out all over her flesh.

"I'm pleased to meet you," Kelvin said. He held out his hand and Josh shook it.

"I guess we should go home and change," Molly said to Josh. She surveyed herself gloomily. "My parents are going to want to know how I got all wet."

"So's my mom," Josh agreed.

"And I never actually asked them if I could go out tonight," Molly added. She was feeling gloomier and gloomier. "They're going to be mad."

"Why should they ever have to know?" Kelvin asked. As Molly and Josh looked at him in puzzlement, he went on, "It'd only make a muckle heap of fuss, and I'd hate to think I caused you two trouble after you tried to save me."

"Well, that's great," Josh replied, sounding annoyed, "but how are we supposed to hide the fact that we're soaked?"

"And cold," Molly put in.

"Running will warm your blood and dry your clothes at the same time," Kelvin said promptly. "And I've a mind to explore this island of yours, if you'll be my guides." He grinned again, his face alight with mischief. "It's a grand night for adventures, I'm thinking."

Adventures! Molly glanced at Josh. It was just what they'd been hoping for.

Then a red ray from the setting sun gleamed into her eye, reminding her that it was almost eight o'clock on a school night. "It's getting late," Molly said reluctantly. "I've got to be home soon."

"Oh, have you a curfew?" Kelvin asked her. He looked sorrowful. "I didn't know. Of course, then, we must get you home. Ah, well, it's fair lonely I'll be tonight, unless . . ." He put a hand on Josh's shoulder. "Do *you* have a curfew, too?"

Josh looked both startled and eager. "No."

"Hey!" Molly said indignantly. So the boys were planning to go ahead and have adventures without her, were they?

"Well, I don't," Josh told her.

"Neither do I," Molly retorted. "I never said I did." And it was true, she told herself. She didn't have a curfew any more than Josh did. Her parents might expect her to be home at a certain time, but they'd never told her she *had* to be home then.

Kelvin laughed. "So no one has a curfew? What are we waiting for, then? Let's be off!"

And he set off, running, down the lake shore.

Almost without thinking, Molly followed. She found herself laughing as she ran, filled with a sudden, wild sense of freedom. Glancing again at Josh, she saw that he felt the same.

Kelvin ran west, toward the last of the sunset. "Up and over!" he called, gesturing toward the low, wooded hill in front of them. "To the sea!"

The three of them pounded through the trees, reaching the hilltop just as the sun disappeared altogether. "There's the moon—and the first star," Kelvin said, pointing. He wasn't even out of breath, Molly thought. "Ah, it'll be a grand, lovely night."

And then he was off again, racing across fields and meadows.

"Stop," Molly gasped at last. "I need to rest. I've never run this far before!"

They'd gone over a mile, judging from where they were now, at the edge of Mrs. Richmond's pasture. Molly was hot and gasping, but she felt wonderful.

"Hey, my clothes are almost dry," Josh marveled, touching his red-and-yellow shorts.

"What did I tell you?" Kelvin laughed. He looked around in the twilight. "Where are we, then?"

"Mrs. Richmond's land," Molly panted.

"Her name's easy to remember because she's really rich," Josh added. He pointed toward a tall black gelding who was eyeing them suspiciously from the other side of a split-rail fence. "That's her horse. I don't think she rides anymore, though."

"She's too fat," Molly put in. She'd caught her breath by now.

But Josh shook his head. "That isn't why. The horse kept throwing her off. And one time it bit her nephew. It's mean."

"Mean? Och, no," Kelvin said. Climbing lightly over the fence, he moved toward the horse, clucking softly at it. The horse's ears swiveled forward.

"Come on, he won't hurt you," Kelvin said over his shoulder to Josh and Molly.

Josh was already over the fence. Molly gulped and went after him. Though she loved horses in theory, the truth was, when she was actually around them she found them a little intimidating. Especially when they were as big as this one!

"Come here, brother," Kelvin said to the horse. As if it understood him, the black gelding trotted to him and nuzzled his shoulder. Kelvin leaned forward and whispered something in the horse's ear.

Whatever he said, it had an incredible effect. The horse flung its head up, let out a neigh, and wheeled around. It thundered past Molly and Josh, straight for the fence, and leaped over in a clean, soaring arc.

Kelvin threw back his head and whooped with delight. "Go on, my friend!" he yelled.

"You made Mrs. Richmond's horse run away!" Molly cried.

"I liberated him," Kelvin corrected. Moonlight picked out a green strand in his dark hair. "It was the only decent thing to do. It sounded a bit of a dull, dreadful life for a self-respecting horse like him."

Molly gaped at him, torn between alarm and exhilaration. He grinned and clapped her shoulder.

"Come on!" he said.

And then they were running again, laughing and whooping, into the cover of the woods.

This time, Molly noticed, they were heading south. "I thought we were going to the sea," she said breathlessly to Kelvin.

"Change of plans," he told her. His brown eyes were luminous. "I've an idea to liberate all the horses."

"*All*?" Molly gasped. "Kelvin, we can't!"

He laughed. "Can't we, now?"

"But . . . but . . ." Molly trailed off. She was too out of breath to argue. Besides, she realized, she didn't know what to say. He couldn't mean it, she told herself. He must be joking!

They reduced their speed to a fast walk. Kelvin led the way, picking a sure path through the shadowy undergrowth.

"I thought we were supposed to be showing him the way around the island," Josh said to Molly. "How does he know where he's going?"

Kelvin must have overheard. "I'm going where

the horses are," he called over his shoulder. "Didn't you hear them neigh?"

Molly and Josh looked at each other.

"I didn't hear any neigh," Molly whispered.

Kelvin swung around. "Ah, but then your ears aren't as sharp as mine," he said. He grinned at the startled expression on Molly's face.

When they emerged from the woods Molly saw they were outside a long, low building with a white-fenced paddock next to it. Behind it bulked a large, gabled house. Her jaw dropped. The Blackberry Island Hunt Club!

"Kelvin, we can't," she protested, grabbing his arm. "I mean, we really can't."

"Why not?" he inquired mildly.

"It's the Hunt Club!" Molly sputtered.

"They'll throw us in jail," Josh added. "They'll shoot us! They'll skin us alive!"

Kelvin held up one finger. "Only if they catch us," he said. "But if you don't want to do it, wait outside. I'll go by myself."

Without a sound, he climbed over the paddock fence and vanished into the stable.

"What do we do?" Molly whispered frantically.

"O'Brien, this is crazy," Josh said.

"I know," she agreed.

"We're going to be in *deep* trouble," Josh added.

Molly nodded. "I know," she said again.

They stared at each other for a moment. Then,

suddenly, Josh grinned. "Well, if we're going to be in trouble anyway, we might as well go for it."

A strange, wild elation bubbled up inside Molly. "Okay. Let's!"

Whisking through the stable door, they let their eyes adjust to the dark for a moment. They saw that Kelvin was unhooking the chains from across each stall door. "Come out, friends," he whispered to the horses inside.

Molly darted to the far end of the stable and began unhooking chains there, while Josh worked from the other end.

Soon the drowsy horses were all milling in the wide aisle that ran down the center of the stable. "Open the big doors at the end," Kelvin directed Molly and Josh. "Then stand clear."

They ran to do it. From her post just inside the stable, Molly could see Kelvin, standing behind the horses, raise his arms. He said some words in a strange language. At the end his voice rose to a shout, and Molly heard something that sounded like "Eh-ack wizzy."

The horses squealed and trumpeted. Then, in one thundering bunch, they pelted out through the open doors and streamed over the paddock fence.

"Hah! Run, friends!" Kelvin cried, following them out. "Scatter! Go! Be free!"

"The clubhouse lights just went on!" Josh said suddenly.

Molly spun around. Josh was right. Two of the windows glowed yellow. More light spilled out as the front door opened.

"Someone's coming," she whispered.

Suddenly the paddock was blindingly lit by a row of floodlights. Molly shrank back into the shadows, flinging up a hand to shield her eyes.

"Oh, no," Josh said. "If we climb over the fence, they'll see our faces."

Molly's heart thudded into her sneakers as she understood what Josh was saying.

They were trapped.

CHAPTER FIVE

Molly put her head in her hands. "Grounded for life," she whispered.

"Who's out there?" called a man's voice from the clubhouse. "Whoever you are, the sheriff is on his way."

"Grounded?" Josh said. "We'll be sent to reform school, more like."

All this time, Kelvin had said nothing, just stood there looking amused. Now he grinned at Josh and Molly. "You two sit tight here," he whispered. "I'll lead them away. Then you can go home, and no one'll be the wiser. There'll be no trouble."

"But what about you?" Molly asked, aghast. "What'll you say if they catch you?"

"They won't," Kelvin said simply. Before Molly

or Josh could say anything more, he darted across the paddock. In the floodlights, his white shirt and red vest showed as plainly as if it were day.

"Hey, kid! Stop!" yelled the voice from the clubhouse. From the stable, Molly and Josh heard heavy footsteps pounding toward the paddock.

Light as a deer, Kelvin vaulted over the fence and ran toward the south. The man from the clubhouse followed, shouting.

As soon as the sound of his voice died away, Molly and Josh came out of their hiding place, quickly climbed the fence, and headed north toward home.

"I hope Kelvin doesn't get caught," Molly said, biting her lip anxiously.

"You know something? I don't think he will," Josh answered. He heaved a sigh. "It's weird. I can't decide whether I like him or hate him. He seems—I don't know, dangerous, somehow."

Molly nodded. "I know. But I don't think he's bad. It's more like he's wild."

"Maybe you're right," Josh said. "I don't know. One thing's for sure, though. Kelvin is definitely different."

The next day at school, everyone was talking about the Hunt Club horses getting out.

"I heard it was a gang of teenagers who let them out," Ann Chiu said at lunch. "I bet it was some of the summer people."

Charlotte Anderson sniffed. "I think the night groom at the club probably forgot to close the paddock gate. My mom says he's a lazy bum. He probably made up that story about the gang of teenagers so he wouldn't get blamed. I hope they fire him."

Molly shifted uncomfortably in her seat. It had never occurred to her that someone *else* might get in trouble for what they had done. She shot a quick glance at Josh, who was sitting at the next table with a bunch of boys. She could tell by his stiff back that he was listening.

"They got all the horses back, right?" she said. "I heard that most of them came back on their own, anyway. So it's not really a big deal, is it? I mean, no one got hurt or anything."

"Not a big deal?" Charlotte huffed. "One of those horses is my mom's. She might never have gotten it back!" Darkly, she added, "*Someone* is going to pay for what happened last night."

Molly swallowed. Maybe it was time to change the subject.

Fortunately, at that moment the bell rang, signaling the end of lunch period. Molly stuffed her sandwich wrapper into her empty milk carton and headed for the trash cans. Josh fell into step beside her.

"Did everything go okay last night?" he asked in a low voice.

Molly nodded. "I snuck in through the shed and went up the back stairs while my parents were in the dining room talking to some guests. They never even noticed I was gone. How about you?"

"It was cool," Josh said. "My mom was out at a meeting of the historical society, and my little brother and sister were at my dad's for the night. So unless one of the neighbors noticed me coming home after ten and tells my mom, I'm fine."

"Good." Molly picked up her books from the lunch table. "I have to go to DeKater Hollow with Charlotte after school to finish the science assignment from yesterday. Maybe you could find Kelvin at his campground and make sure he's okay."

"I'll go there after b-ball. Hey, how'd you get Charlotte to agree to go with you to DeKater Hollow?" Josh asked curiously. "I thought it was a toss-up which she hated more, you or schoolwork."

Molly's brows drew together in a puzzled frown. "You know, I didn't even wonder about that," she said slowly. "It *is* weird. I wonder what made her agree to come with me."

At four-thirty that afternoon, Molly got her answer.

The two girls had agreed to meet at DeKater Hollow, since Charlotte said she had things to do after school. When Molly saw her, it was clear what those things had been.

"Oh, brother," Molly groaned as Charlotte walked toward her.

Earlier that day Charlotte been wearing plain jeans and a polo shirt. Now she had on a pink-and-white-striped shorts set that made her look like a candy cane, in Molly's opinion. Her chestnut hair had obviously been curled, and as she came closer Molly began to suspect that she was actually wearing makeup. At least, she'd never noticed before that Charlotte had glittery green eyelids and streaks of pink on each cheekbone.

"Is . . . anyone else here?" Charlotte asked in a casual voice.

"If you mean Kelvin, I haven't seen him," Molly answered dryly.

"Who? Oh, that Scottish kid." Charlotte's blush-covered cheeks turned a shade redder. "I forgot about him."

"Oh, sure," Molly muttered.

Charlotte's eyes narrowed. "Well, I'm here," she said irritably. "What do you want me to do?"

"We need to find two more animals to finish yesterday's assignment, and then we need to work on our report," Molly said. She was glad to change the subject. If Charlotte spent all her time thinking about seeing Kelvin, they'd never get their work done.

"Okay." Charlotte set out along the lake shore—in the direction of the marshy spot where Kelvin had been the day before. Oh, well, as long as they finished their work, it didn't matter if Charlotte wasted some time flirting. Anyway, Molly wouldn't mind seeing Kelvin herself, to make sure he was all right.

It was a gusty day. Wind whipped the lake's surface into small whitecaps and tousled Charlotte's carefully arranged hair, to Molly's secret glee.

As they passed the place where the boats were, Molly's eyes caught a flash of orange hovering by the water's edge. "Look," she called to Charlotte. "One animal down, one to go. There's a monarch butterfly."

"Whoopee," Charlotte said in a bored voice.

Ignoring that comment, Molly pulled out her notebook and started jotting down a description of the delicate insect. "It's so pretty! I wish I could draw. It'd make a great illustration for our report," she said.

"I can draw," Charlotte said.

"You can?" Molly stared at her in surprise. "Will you draw it?"

"Okay," Charlotte agreed. For once there was no hostility in her voice. In fact, she almost sounded eager, as if she were glad to be asked. Pulling out her own notebook and a pencil, she perched on one of the overturned canoes and began to sketch.

After a few moments, Molly came and peered over Charlotte's shoulder. She was impressed by the way the butterfly had taken shape under Charlotte's delicate pencil strokes. "Wow, that's really good," she said admiringly. "You're so lucky to be able to draw like that."

"I always get A's in art," Charlotte said. But she didn't sound smug.

"Not me. I'm awful at it," Molly admitted. "It's the only class I ever got a C in." Leaning down, she pointed to the eyes Charlotte had just finished sketching in on the butterfly. "But even a terrible artist like me can tell you that butterflies don't have long curly eyelashes," she said, laughing.

She was taken aback when Charlotte rounded on her with a scowl. "Fine, brainiac, you draw it, then," Charlotte said. "I was just trying to make it look nice."

"It does look nice," Molly protested. "It's just not accurate, that's all. It needs to be accurate for a science report."

"Science is for losers," Charlotte said, tossing her head.

Stung, Molly retorted, "You're the one who's going to be a loser if you fail this class!"

All the sullenness came back into Charlotte's face. Her lips set into a thin line and she glared at Molly.

Oh, brother! Molly said to herself. Now everything was ruined, just when it had seemed that she and Charlotte might actually be able to declare a truce between them.

"Yoo-hoo!" A boy's voice drifted over the water. "Hello, girls!"

Charlotte's and Molly's heads both jerked up at the sound. Molly squinted out over the glare on the lake. Near its center, she could just make out a dark head bobbing on the choppy surface.

"It's him!" Charlotte said excitedly.

Molly's eyebrows rose. It *was* Kelvin. But where had he come from? DeKater Lake wasn't that big. Why hadn't she seen him coming down to the water's edge, even if he was on the far shore?

"Come on out," Kelvin was shouting.

Charlotte jumped up and began trying to turn over the beached canoe she'd been sitting on. "Help me," she ordered Molly. "Let's go out there!"

"We can't take this canoe," Molly objected. "It isn't ours."

"We're just borrowing it, stupid," Charlotte said impatiently. "Don't be such a goody-goody."

Molly flushed. She hated to be called that! Anyway, surely using someone else's canoe was no worse than liberating the horses had been, last night. . . .

"Aren't you coming?" Kelvin called.

"Come on!" Charlotte said to Molly.

Setting her chin, Molly seized hold of the canoe and helped Charlotte flip it over. Together the two girls slid it to the water's edge. Molly stood up to her ankles in the shallows, holding the slender craft steady while Charlotte climbed into the bow. Then she got in herself, took a paddle from under the seat, and shoved off.

Too late, she remembered that she still had her knapsack, full of a new supply of library books, with her. She couldn't paddle with that on her back. She unslung it and put it in the bottom of the canoe, hoping that the boat didn't leak.

It didn't, but that didn't make Molly feel much better. Charlotte had no idea of how to behave in a canoe. She kept moving around, leaning over to check her reflection in the water, and tossing her head to fluff up her hair. "Charlotte, *please* sit still," Molly begged as the light craft nearly tipped over for the third time.

Charlotte paid her no attention. "Can't we make this thing go faster?" she demanded.

Suddenly a strong gust of wind swept the lake, rocking the canoe. Charlotte let go of her paddle and clutched both hands to her head. "My hair!" she complained.

"The paddle!" Molly groaned. The discarded oar was drifting slowly away from the canoe.

"Oh, don't worry, Kelvin can get it for us," Charlotte said carelessly. Another gust struck the canoe and she grasped the side with one hand, holding her hair down with the other. "I can't believe this wind. It's *wrecking* my hair."

Molly gazed around, feeling a bit uneasy. The wind was doing more than just ruffling their hair, she noticed. It was starting to make sizable waves on DeKater Lake. Waves that could not only soak all her library books, but could even, possibly, swamp their canoe.

"Oh, he's over there," Charlotte squealed, pointing. "Row us that way," she commanded Molly. "Kelvin!"

"I can't row us that way until you sit still," Molly said shortly.

But Charlotte paid no attention to her. "He can't hear me. Kelvin!" she yelled again. Then she stood up—just as the strongest puff of wind yet slammed against their canoe.

"Charlotte, *sit*!" Molly screamed.

But it was too late. The canoe rocked left, then right. Charlotte teetered, shrieking.

They were going over.

CHAPTER SIX

Everything seemed to be happening with extraordinary deliberation. Molly felt as if she'd suddenly gone into a slow-motion world.

The canoe heeled left, and above her the sky swung in a dizzy arc the opposite way. Suddenly Molly was on a slant, staring at a foam-flecked wall of greenish water that was rushing toward her. It was a wave, she realized. And it was about to break over her head, swamping the canoe and very likely washing her knapsack away. All because of that idiot Charlotte.

Suddenly Molly was supremely annoyed. "No!" she yelled at the top of her lungs.

For a split second, the wave stopped.

It wasn't much, but it was enough time for the

canoe to right itself, rock to the right, and begin swinging back to the left. At that instant the wave broke harmlessly against the metal side. The canoe's rocking quickly petered out. Molly's mouth fell open in awe.

A shaking Charlotte resumed her seat in the prow. "Oh, wow, we almost drowned," she babbled.

"Did you see that?" Molly demanded. "Did you see? The water stopped when I yelled!"

"What are you talking about?" Charlotte asked scornfully.

"Indeed, it sounds as if she thinks she has power over the water," Kelvin's voice said agreeably. His dark, wet head, sleek as a seal, appeared by Charlotte's right knee. He was treading water so smoothly that you couldn't tell he was moving at all.

Charlotte's hands flew to fix her hair. "Hi," she said breathlessly.

"Hello," Kelvin said, smiling at her. "Are you enjoying your ride, then?"

Charlotte rolled her eyes. "In this dinky canoe? Boy, you should see my dad's speedboat. Now *that's* fun. It goes so fast!"

"Speedboats are just stinkpots," Molly muttered. "I think they should be banned." She hated the stench of diesel fuel and the noise of the engines. It figured Charlotte would like power boats.

Kelvin raised his eyebrows at Molly. "Do you? And do you also think you can control the waves?"

Charlotte snickered.

Molly's face felt hot. Okay, so maybe she had imagined the whole thing. Maybe it did sound stupid, too. But did Kelvin have to make fun of her in front of Charlotte?

"Never mind," she muttered.

"Did you see how we almost tipped over?" Charlotte asked him. "If I had fallen in the water, you would have saved me, wouldn't you?"

At the syrupy note in her voice, Molly rolled her eyes.

Kelvin propped an arm on the side of the canoe. "Och, now, I don't know about that," he said gravely.

For a second Charlotte's blue eyes were round with surprise. Then she laughed, but Molly thought it seemed a little forced.

"You're funny," Charlotte told Kelvin.

He smiled. "Thank you."

Charlotte giggled. Molly gritted her teeth. If she gets any more goopy, I might just tip the boat over myself, she thought irritably. She gave Kelvin a sour look. Clearly, he hadn't come to any harm as a result of their adventures last night.

"Charlotte, we better go finish the science assignment. It's due Friday, don't forget," she said. "It's almost six now. I have to be home for dinner at seven, and it would be great if we could start writing our report before then."

Charlotte tore her attention away from Kelvin

long enough to shoot Molly an irritated look. "Well, I can't. I have to go home *now*," she said.

Molly's hands tightened on her paddle, but she kept her temper. "Okay, then maybe we can work after dinner," she said evenly. "Can you come over to my house later?"

Charlotte looked as if she was about to say no. Then she darted a look at Kelvin, who had been watching the exchange with interest.

"Okay," she said quickly. "I'll get my mom to drive me over at eight."

Molly had to be satisfied with that.

Kelvin obligingly swam over and fetched the paddle Charlotte had dropped, but he declined to go ashore with the two girls. "I left my things over on the other shore," he explained. "See you later." And he dived under the water's surface.

Molly and Charlotte paddled the canoe back in silence. Charlotte had sunk into the same dreamy state she'd been in after meeting Kelvin the previous day. Molly, glad not to have to suffer her sarcastic remarks, left her alone.

As they beached the canoe, Molly scanned the lake and the far shore for Kelvin. But, as before, there was no sign of him. It was as if he vanished into thin air, or melted into the water, she thought. How did he do it?

Puzzled, she shouldered her knapsack and started for home.

* * *

As she put her books down on the kitchen table, the phone rang. "Molly, it's Josh," Gwen yelled from the second floor.

Mrs. O'Brien, who was coming through from the dining room, frowned. "Take it upstairs, and remind your sister not to yell when we have guests in the dining room," she told Molly.

Molly bounded up the back stairs and grabbed the phone from Gwen's hand. "Mom says don't yell," she said. Then, into the phone, she added, "Boy, wait till you hear about my afternoon!"

"Hey, O'Brien," Josh said. "For once, will you let me talk first?"

"Oh," Molly said, a bit taken aback. "Sorry."

"No big deal," Josh said. "Listen, I found out something weird this afternoon. About Kelvin."

"Really? What?"

"Well, I went to find him at the campground, like you suggested. You know, the camp at Chapin Bay where those English kids have been staying."

"He wasn't there," Molly said. She wrapped the phone cord around her finger. "I saw him at DeKater Hollow. He's okay. But, Josh, you won't believe what happened! There was this wave, see—"

"O'Brien," Josh interrupted. "Can I finish?"

"Sorry," Molly said meekly.

"I asked a bunch of the English kids if they knew where Kelvin was. Know what? None of them knew

64

who I was talking about. They'd never even heard of him."

Molly frowned. "That *is* weird. How could they not know who he is when he's with their group?"

"Don't be dense," Josh said. "Don't you get it? He *isn't* with their group. He lied."

"You're the one who's being dense," Molly retorted indignantly. "Why on earth would Kelvin lie about something like that? I bet you pronounced his name funny, and the English kids just didn't understand you."

"Uh-uh. I even described him," Josh said. "Face it, O'Brien. I know he's supposed to be so cute, and I know all you girls are gaga over him and his stupid accent—"

"I am not!" Molly sputtered.

"But the truth is," Josh went on, "there's something fishy about the guy. He doesn't add up."

Molly opened her mouth to make an angry reply, then shut it again. She had to admit there was some truth in what Josh said. Kelvin *didn't* add up. He came out of nowhere, he seemed able to vanish into nowhere, and no one knew anything about him.

Then she thought of something. "He never actually said he was one of the English campers," she said slowly. "Charlotte just assumed he was, and he never told her she was wrong."

"Okay, so he didn't actually lie," Josh said. "But I still want to know: If he isn't one of the English campers, then who *is* he?"

By Thursday morning, Molly had found other things to worry about. Working with Charlotte the night before had been frustrating. Charlotte seemed to have absorbed little of what they'd learned in Ms. Groening's class that year, and to care even less.

Molly had ended up writing one of their two reports by herself, after Charlotte went home. That left the other still to be written today, and then they had to type both reports into Charlotte's computer. Molly wasn't sure how they were going to get it all done.

But that wasn't all. As she brushed her teeth, Molly thought about Charlotte's notes from the field trip. When Molly had asked to see the notes, Charlotte hadn't wanted to hand them over. And when she finally did, Molly had seen why she was so reluctant.

Although Charlotte's handwriting was nice, her spelling, grammar, and punctuation were horrible. "It's lefs have pupel strips," Molly had read. It took her a moment to figure out that the sentence was supposed to read "Its leaves have purple stripes." She'd been about to say something, but the look on Charlotte's face had warned her to keep her mouth shut.

Molly pulled on a pair of overalls and went down to the kitchen, where Gwen was already eating breakfast. She could hear her father talking on the business phone in the study. "All right, Mr. Halleck, I understand," he was saying. "No, you certainly can't be blamed. Right, thanks for calling. So long."

A moment later David O'Brien came into the kitchen. He was frowning. "It's the strangest thing," he told the girls. "Ned Halleck just called to tell me he won't be able to supply the lobsters I ordered for tonight's dinner. There isn't a lobster to be had on all of Blackberry Island. It seems someone went around to all the pots last night and let the lobsters out."

Kelvin! Molly nearly choked on a spoonful of oatmeal. It had to have been him.

"Did—did anyone see who did it?" she asked.

"Well, Vernon Baker said he saw a teenage boy in a red vest hanging around his boat last night," Mr. O'Brien said. "But I don't know how one kid could have done something like that on his own. It would take hours to haul up all those pots and let the lobsters out. Besides, Vernon's boat was out of fuel, so the boy couldn't have taken it out."

"Maybe the boy had a group of helpers," Gwen suggested. "And maybe they had scuba-diving stuff, so they didn't have to use a boat at all. They just swam underwater and opened all the traps."

Mr. O'Brien laughed. "I'll have to mention that theory to the sheriff next time I see him."

"Does the sheriff think the boy in the red vest is the one who did it?" Molly persisted.

"Who knows if Vernon even told him about the boy?" her father said. "I'm sure the sheriff knows it could have been anyone. Especially now that the island's overrun with summer people."

Molly slumped in her seat, feeling relieved. She didn't know exactly what to think of Kelvin, but she knew she'd feel bad if he got caught.

Mr. O'Brien broke into her thoughts. "It's raining," he announced, peering out the window. "And the fog is setting in. Come on, girls, get your books and I'll drive you to school."

"I can't believe Charlotte," Molly muttered aloud. "She stood me up!" She hung up the pay phone and glared at it.

It was four o'clock on Thursday afternoon. Charlotte was supposed to have met Molly at the library a half hour earlier, but she had never showed up. And when Molly called her house, no one answered the phone.

It figured, Molly thought bitterly. Now she'd have to write the report by herself. Again.

Rain fell in a thin, spitting drizzle as she turned and went into the Blackberry Island library. Her jaw set with anger, she laid her books out at a table and got to work.

Two hours later, she stood up and rubbed a crick out of her neck. "Done," she said aloud.

"Shh," said the elderly librarian.

"Sorry," Molly whispered, and gathered her things together.

She was still mad at Charlotte for skipping their meeting, but now that her temper had had time to cool, she began to think that maybe it wasn't all bad. If Charlotte had showed up, Molly would have had to put up with her rudeness and lack of interest. Also, whatever writing Charlotte had done, Molly probably would have had to do over, and that would have made Charlotte angry—and even meaner than usual.

She wouldn't say anything to Ms. Groening about how awful Charlotte had been, Molly decided. She didn't want to be a tattletale. But Charlotte could definitely do all the typing!

The decision made her feel better. She hurried out and made her way through the warm, foggy evening to the Andersons' big brick house.

Mrs. Anderson answered the door. She was a big woman in expensive-looking clothes, with the same chestnut hair and cold blue eyes as Charlotte.

"Oh, you're the one whose parents bought that awful old inn," she said when Molly introduced herself. "Charlotte isn't here."

Molly suppressed an indignant retort. "Could I leave these for her?" she asked, holding up the reports. "They're for our science project. She's going to type them on your computer."

Mrs. Anderson took the reports. "I'll give them

to her," she said carelessly. "Oh, and, Polly—is that your name?—tell your parents that if they're ever in the market for a *decent* piece of property, they should call me. I'm a real estate agent, you know."

"I'll tell them," Molly mumbled.

What a horrible person! she thought as the door closed behind Mrs. Anderson. Now she knew where Charlotte got it!

When Molly got home she saw Grandpa Lloyd's truck in the parking area behind the inn. Since the inn's restaurant had become successful, Grandpa Lloyd didn't come over as often as he used to. Molly missed seeing him all the time. So it was nice to find him in the kitchen, chopping up mushrooms and Italian sausage.

"Your folks drafted me into making supper for you kids," he told Molly. "What do you say to homemade pizza?"

"All right!" she cheered. "Can I help?"

It was a great dinner. Molly stuffed herself with pizza. Then, her stomach full and her mind finally free from worry about the science project, she left Gwen and Andrew to clean up and went to her room to read the books Uncle Jack had sent.

The books lay on her desk, by the black Sithstone. When Molly picked up the stone, it shot through her fingers to the floor. She'd forgotten its odd, slippery texture. Stooping, she retrieved it.

The carvings on the front of the stone looked like runes. They were probably fake, she thought. Too bad. It would have been so cool if the stone really did give her power over one of the Sith!

Putting the stone back on her desk, she picked up *Myths and Folktales from the Scottish Islands* and lay down on her bed to read.

By ten o'clock she had worked her way through giants, ogres, and dragons to the section on water spirits. "The Kelpie, or Water Horse" was the title of the first story.

She started to read. "In the days of King Malcolm, the bonniest maid on all of Skye was Donald MacNeill's daughter, Gruoch of the golden hair," the story began. "Every man who saw her loved her, and none more than Findlaech, the sorcerer's boy. But Gruoch was proud and cold. She laughed at Findlaech, and told him: 'Sooner will I marry a troll or a kelpie than you, boy, penniless as you are.'

"Then Findlaech's heart was sore, and he said, 'Be careful what you wish for, for it may come to pass.' And that night in his master's house he read long in the great book of spells. And the people saw flames flickering behind the windows, though it was midsummer.

"The next day a stranger came to Skye. He was handsome as a prince, with broad shoulders and flashing dark eyes, and long hair black as midnight, but coarse like a horse's tail. When Gruoch saw him, she fell instantly in love."

"Uh-oh," Molly murmured. She could guess what was coming next. The dark stranger must be the water horse, or kelpie. Whatever it was, it was magical. And whatever was going to happen to the proud, cruel Gruoch, it couldn't be good. Flipping over onto her stomach, Molly propped her chin on her hands and started reading again.

Just then there were three slow, deliberate taps at the window. Molly's heart jumped into her throat. Was something out there?

Slowly she turned her head, her brown eyes wide, and looked over her shoulder at the window. She nearly screamed.

Staring back in at her was a ghostly face.

CHAPTER SEVEN

Molly leaped off the bed, her heart beating wildly.

The face's mouth moved. "It's me, Kelvin." His voice came faintly through the glass. "Are you going to open the window, then?"

"Kelvin!" Molly exclaimed. Hurrying to the window, she slid it up. "What in the world are you doing? How did you get up here?"

"Do you mean to say you've never tried climbing up to your window before? Och, it's great fun you've missed," Kelvin said.

Molly gulped. She hadn't even known it could be done! There was nothing to stand on but a narrow ledge where the rain gutter ran under her window. And he must have climbed up the rickety metal downspout. It was incredible that it hadn't collapsed under his weight.

"You're crazy," she told him.

"Am I?" Kelvin propped his elbows on the sill, smiling as though his presence were the most natural thing in the world. Wisps of mist drifted through the open window. His hair was beaded with moisture, she saw. And mixed in among the dark strands were bits of green water-weed. Didn't he ever comb his hair after he went swimming?

Molly folded her arms. "Anyway, I'm glad you're here," she said. "I have a lot of questions for you."

"Do you? Well, I've but one for you, so let me ask it first," Kelvin said. His eyes glimmered with mischief. "Will you come out again with me?"

"What—now?" Molly was astounded. "Tonight?"

"Aye, when else?"

"But . . . but what would we do?"

"Who knows?" Kelvin flung his arms wide.

Molly gasped. "Be careful! You could fall!"

"I could," Kelvin agreed, leaning on the sill again. His teeth flashed white as he smiled. "As it happens, I didn't. But you never know. You see? Half the adventure lies in not knowing."

Molly's skin prickled with excitement. She did see, when he said it like that. But . . .

"I can't go out this late," she argued. "My parents will never let me."

"Then don't ask," he said. "Come down the way

74

I came up. You'll come to no harm, I promise."

Molly was suddenly full of longing to go with Kelvin, to try her luck in climbing down from her window, to run through the mist, to do all the things she'd never done before. But did she dare?

"What about Josh?" she asked.

"We'll fetch him next," Kelvin promised. His liquid brown eyes seemed to glow with their own light. "Are you with me, then?"

There was a knock on her door. "Molly?" her mother's voice called. "Can I come in?"

"Mom!" Molly yelped. She spun around just as the door opened and Mrs. O'Brien walked in.

"I thought I heard voices," Mrs. O'Brien said. She gave her daughter a quizzical smile. "Have you been talking to yourself?"

Nailed! Molly's cheeks turned scarlet. She considered herself pretty good at handling her parents under ordinary circumstances, but there was no way in the world she'd be able to explain the wild boy at her window in a way that would satisfy her mother.

The only thing to do was to take the bull by the horns. Molly cleared her throat. "Uh, Mom," she said, turning to the window. "This is—"

Then she broke off, astonished. There was no one outside the window.

Kelvin was gone.

* * *

The next day at school, Molly caught up with Josh at his locker right before lunch.

"What's up?" Josh asked. "You look tired. Were you working late on your science project?"

"Oh, that." Molly had practically forgotten about the project. "I finished it before dinner. Unless Charlotte messed up the typing, we're home free. No, I was up late"—she glanced around, then lowered her voice— "because of Kelvin."

"What happened?" Josh asked softly.

Molly told him how Kelvin had climbed up to her window and tried to get her to come out. "I would have gone, too, if my mom hadn't come into my room," Molly said. "I don't know how he does it, but when I'm around him I feel like I can do anything, and there's no such thing as right or wrong."

"I know what you mean," Josh agreed. He frowned in thought. "I wonder what he ended up doing last night."

Molly winced. "Don't you get the feeling we'll find out soon enough?"

And they did, a few minutes later, as they walked past the principal's office on their way to the lunchroom.

Just as they passed the door, Mr. LaGamba, the vice-principal, came storming out, followed by an anxious-looking secretary. "Someone's going to pay for this!" Mr. LaGamba bellowed, then disappeared down the hall and out the front door.

"Oh, dear." The secretary, a round, rosy elderly woman, wrung her hands. "Oh, dear!"

"What's wrong, Mrs. Bonniface?" Josh asked. "Why is Mr. LaGamba so upset?"

"Oh, well, it's his boat," the secretary replied. "It was brand-new last summer, and he was so *proud* of it . . . oh, dear."

"What happened to his boat?" Molly persisted. Mrs. Bonniface was really nice, but sometimes it took a while for her to get to the point.

Mrs. Bonniface looked startled. "Why, the same thing that happened to all the other boats on Blackberry Island. Haven't you heard?"

Molly and Josh exchanged a quick glance. "No," she said. "Tell us, please."

"Gone," Mrs. Bonniface said, spreading her arms. "Set adrift from the docks and the moorings during the night."

"Every single boat?" Molly gasped.

"Except the sailboats," Mrs. Bonniface said. "And, of course, the ferries weren't docked, so they were left alone. And I don't think any of the fishing trawlers were touched, either." She frowned. "Now that you mention it, I believe it was just the speedboats, in fact."

Molly gulped, remembering the conversation with Kelvin and Charlotte when she'd said she thought speedboats ought to be banned. Maybe she was being paranoid, but she had to wonder if her words had given Kelvin the idea.

"Oh, boy," Josh muttered as they walked away. "First he liberates the horses. Then the lobsters. Now he liberates the speedboats! What's next?"

Molly shook her head helplessly. "I don't know. I don't think he knows, either. He's like—he's like a hurricane, or some other natural disaster."

"Except that natural disasters can't be caught by the sheriff and sent to reform school," Josh pointed out.

Molly bit her lip, then asked, "Josh, I know it's weird to be thinking this way about someone who's older than we are . . . but do you think we should talk to him, set him straight? I mean, freeing horses and lobsters is one thing, but cutting loose a lot of boats is something else. People might not get them back, and boats cost a lot of money. I don't think he understands how much trouble he could be in."

"I doubt if it would do much good to talk to him," Josh answered. "You know how Kelvin has this way of answering a question with another question? If he doesn't feel like discussing something, it's like talking to a brick wall."

Molly nodded. She knew just what Josh meant.

"But," he said as they entered the cafeteria, "maybe we *should* try. What do we have to lose?"

"Let's look for him after school," Molly suggested.

"Right." Josh headed for his usual table. "See you later."

During lunch Molly looked for Charlotte, but she wasn't in the cafeteria. Molly felt a prickle of worry. "I hope Charlotte isn't out sick today," she said to Ann Chiu. "She has our project."

"Oh, no, she's here," Ann assured Molly. "I saw her this morning, and she was carrying the report in one of those clear binders. She said she had to finish working on something during lunch."

"Great!" Molly ate the rest of her sandwich, pleased. So the project was done, and she'd gotten through the whole thing with Charlotte without any major disasters!

Ann frowned. "She's been really weird this week. Do you know what's wrong with her?"

Molly thought of Kelvin. "Uh—no," she said hastily. Fortunately, the bell rang just then, so she didn't have to say more. Tossing back the last of her milk, she stood up. "Got to go—see you," she said, and hurried away.

Science wasn't till last period that day, and Molly slipped in a moment after the bell rang, because she had had to get a book out of her locker. She gazed around anxiously for Charlotte, then spotted her on the other side of the room. Charlotte gave Molly a single, cold look, then faced front.

What had she done now? Molly wondered. What reason could Charlotte have to be mad at her?

"Okay," Ms. Groening called. "We're going to

start presenting our projects today, and continue through Monday's and Tuesday's classes. How about some volunteers? Who wants to start?"

Molly sat back. She wasn't about to raise her hand. She and Charlotte hadn't had time to prepare a presentation, and she hated having to talk in class without being prepared. It made her freeze. She sighed, realizing she'd have to spend at least an hour working on the presentation with Charlotte over the weekend.

Suddenly, to her horror, she realized that Ms. Groening was calling her name. "Molly?" the teacher said, smiling. "Come on up. Your partner has volunteered your team to go first."

Molly's eyes widened in horror. "But I—" she said. She shot a bewildered look at Charlotte. In return, Charlotte gave her a malicious smile.

Molly's heart was pounding as she made her way up the aisle to the front of the class. "We can't do this now," she told Charlotte in a furious whisper. "We aren't ready."

"I am," Charlotte said smugly. She fanned a sheaf of pencil drawings. That must have been what she was working on during lunch, Molly guessed.

"But I don't have anything to say," Molly protested.

"Come on, Molly," Ms. Groening said. There was a touch of impatience in her voice. "We have a lot to get through today."

Molly took a deep breath. "Ms. Groening, we aren't ready to do our presentation," she admitted. Her cheeks were hot. She'd never had to tell a teacher she wasn't ready before. It felt bad.

"Speak for yourself," Charlotte retorted. "I did the work!"

"Charlotte, what do you mean?" Ms. Groening asked sharply.

There was a short silence. Charlotte licked her lips. Her eyes darted up to Ms. Groening's face, then down again.

"Ms. Groening," she declared, "I did all the work on this project. Molly didn't do a thing!"

CHAPTER EIGHT

Molly stared at Charlotte in total disbelief. *"What?"* she said.

Ms. Groening looked very serious. "Girls, I think you'd better stay after class and talk to me," she said quietly. "Go to your seats now."

The rest of the class passed in a sort of daze for Molly. She spent most of it staring in shock and growing anger at the back of Charlotte's head. How could Charlotte have said such a thing? And did she really think Molly would let her get away with it?

Finally the bell rang and the rest of the seventh-graders filed out. Josh gave her the thumbs-up as he passed her desk. "Good luck," he whispered. "I'll meet you at DeKater Hollow."

Molly nodded and took a deep breath.

"All right," Ms. Groening said when the three of them were alone. She came around to the front of her desk and leaned against it with her arms crossed. "Who wants to start?"

Molly looked at Charlotte, who was staring down at her desk with a sullen, rebellious expression on her face. She knew she wasn't going to get away with it, Molly realized.

"Molly didn't do her share of the work on the science project," Charlotte muttered.

"How can you say that?" Molly burst out. "I had to drag you out to DeKater Hollow to collect samples, and then you practically drowned us in a canoe. And you *know* I did all the writing on the reports. You can't even—"

She broke off. She'd been about to blurt out that Charlotte couldn't spell or punctuate, but something made her stop.

It must be terribly embarrassing for Charlotte not to be able to spell at her age. She was the oldest kid in the seventh grade. She had turned thirteen way back in the fall. In fact, hadn't she heard once that Charlotte had been left back? Maybe that's why she hates me, Molly thought. I *am* good at school. I even skipped a grade.

Lifting her head, she saw that both Ms. Groening and Charlotte were looking at her. On Charlotte's face was a strange blend of appeal and dislike. She didn't want Molly to say anything about her awful spelling, Molly guessed.

It didn't really make any difference. Ms. Groening must know already. But Molly returned Charlotte's look steadily, letting her know that she would keep her mouth shut.

"Well, Charlotte?" Ms. Groening said. "Is Molly telling the truth?"

Charlotte bit her lip. "She did do some of the writing," she muttered at last. "But she stuck me with all the typing. And I had to do it by myself. She wasn't even there."

"Well, you had to do *something*," Molly retorted, her indignation flaring again.

"Show me your reports," Ms. Groening said, holding out her hand.

Charlotte handed over a plastic folder. Ms. Groening read the first couple of paragraphs, then flipped through the report in silence for a few moments. At last she looked up.

"There are some lovely drawings in here," she said. "Did you do those, Charlotte?"

Charlotte looked taken aback. "Y-yes."

"They're excellent," Ms. Groening said. "And the report looks promising, too. I think we can call the project a team effort. But you girls have a few things to talk over, don't you? About giving proper credit." She looked at Charlotte. Then she shifted her gaze to Molly. "And about making more of an effort to be a real team."

Neither Molly nor Charlotte answered. Molly was stiff with resentment. She wouldn't embarrass Charlotte in front of the teacher, she thought. But after all she'd put up with, she sure wasn't about to kiss and make up! Wasn't Ms. Groening going to punish Charlotte for making trouble?

"I had hoped you two might learn something from working with each other, but I think my experiment backfired," Ms. Groening said, as if to herself. Sighing, she addressed the girls. "All right, that's all. You can present your report to the class on Monday. Have a nice weekend."

Gathering her books, Molly hurried out.

As she walked along, she began to feel madder and madder. By the time she reached DeKater Hollow and spotted Josh and Kelvin under the big butternut tree, she was steaming.

"You're not going to believe it," she burst out as soon as she was within earshot. "Charlotte got away with it!"

"You mean Ms. Groening believed Charlotte really did all the work?" Josh demanded.

"No." Molly waved a hand impatiently. "She knows Charlotte lied, but she's not going to punish her or anything. Ooh, I'm so mad I could scream!"

"You are screaming," Josh pointed out.

Molly clenched her fists. "If Charlotte was here right now, I'd punch her in the nose," she said.

"Really?" Kelvin looked interested. "Shall I go

and find her for you, then?"

Molly ignored that. "I just can't believe her!" she fumed. "She's probably going to get the best grade of her life because of me, and she still tries to stab me in the back. I should have told Ms. Groening about her pathetic spelling. I should have told the whole school."

Josh snorted. "Maybe you should save time and just broadcast it on the radio. That way you could reach everyone at once."

"I should!" Molly agreed. "Or maybe I should take out an ad in the paper." She narrowed her eyes. "And *then* I'll punch her in the nose," she added darkly.

The three of them sat in silence for a moment. Then Josh said, "Do you feel better now?"

"A little," Molly told him.

"Well," Josh said, getting to his feet, "I better go. I have stuff to do at home."

"Me, too," Molly said with a sigh. She stood.

Kelvin stared at her. "You mean, after all that, you're not going to do anything to Charlotte?" he asked.

"'Do anything'? You mean, am I really going to punch her in the nose or something?"

"Or something," Kelvin agreed.

"Of course not," Molly said, shocked.

"Oh, I suppose I'll have to do it for you, then," he said cheerfully.

Molly laughed. "Right," she said. "See you later, Kelvin. Bye, Josh."

It wasn't until she was almost home that she remembered that she and Josh had never had their talk with Kelvin after all.

The next morning, Molly lay in bed late, finishing the story of Gruoch and the kelpie. As she suspected, the dark stranger was indeed the kelpie, a kind of water spirit that could take the form of either a horse or a man. This one turned himself into a coal-black horse and enticed Gruoch to get on his back. Then he promptly ran away with her to the sea and plunged in. She was never seen again.

Creepy! Molly thought. Picking up the book of Celtic legends, she flipped to "kelpie."

That book seemed to take a lighter view of kelpies, describing them as mischief-makers and rogues. Their favorite activity was letting people ride them and then dumping them in the nearest lake or river. It didn't say whether the people drowned or just got a good dunking. But the book claimed you could always recognize a kelpie by its mane, which was full of sand or bits of seaweed.

"Molly," her mother called up the stairs. "It's after ten. Are you going to sleep all day, or do you want the French toast I made?"

French toast! "Coming," Molly yelled. Dressing quickly, she ran downstairs.

Gwen and Andrew had gone into town early with Mr. O'Brien, so she was alone with her mother. As she was eating, Grandpa Lloyd came in.

"Hi, Dad," Mrs. O'Brien hailed him. "I thought you'd be out fishing today."

"Naw," Grandpa said. "Marvin LaGamba borrowed my fishing skiff to go out and get his speedboat. Someone spotted it drifting near South Light."

Mrs. O'Brien made a wry face. "I can't deny I have some sympathy for whoever cut all the speedboats loose. There are times when I've wanted to do it myself. Still, I suppose there are better ways to express an opinion. Do they have any idea who did it?"

"Ran into the sheriff this morning. He said he had a lead," Grandpa replied.

Molly sat up a little straighter in her chair. "What kind of lead?" she asked.

Grandpa scratched his ear. "Well, he seems to think there's a connection between all the things that have been happening lately. The night the horses got out, the Hunt Club fellow reported seeing a dark-haired teenage boy in a red vest in the paddock. And the night the lobster pots were opened, Vern Baker saw a young fellow of the same description near his boat."

Molly's throat closed.

"Now, no one claims to have seen this boy the

night the boats were cut loose," Grandpa went on, "but the sheriff figures it's worth talking to him anyway. A couple of kids have reported seeing a boy like that hanging around DeKater Hollow. So the sheriff's going there now to try to find him."

"Oh," Molly said.

"There's more French toast, Molly," her mother said. "Want to finish it?"

"Uh—no, thanks," Molly said. "I'm full."

Her mother looked surprised. "After one piece of French toast? Are you feeling all right?"

Molly squirmed in her seat. "I'm fine. I'm just not that hungry. Can I be excused?"

"Of course," Mrs. O'Brien said, shrugging.

As Molly slid out of her seat, Grandpa Lloyd gave her a sharp look. He said nothing. But Molly, hurrying toward the front door, wondered if he suspected where she was going. Somehow, Grandpa seemed able to figure things out, even when other adults didn't have a clue.

Once she was outside, she ran. She took the shortcut to DeKater Hollow, turning off the road and down an old, overgrown lane, then slithering down a steep, wooded hill.

By the time she came to the bottom of the hill, Molly was thoroughly winded. But she didn't stop. There was no time to catch her breath. She had to warn Kelvin before the sheriff found him.

Far ahead, by the reeds where she'd first met

Kelvin, she caught sight of something black moving through the water. Her eyes widened and she came to a stop as she realized it was a horse.

Had Mrs. Richmond's gelding escaped again? Molly wondered. This horse looked grander, somehow, than the gelding, but she couldn't see it well enough at this distance to be sure of its identity.

The horse was in the shallows now. Its magnificent black coat glistened in the sun. It tossed its head, and a rainbow of water sprayed from its heavy mane. Then it trotted into the reeds. With an odd feeling of suspense, Molly stepped back into the trees and waited to see what happened next.

A moment later, the reeds parted and Kelvin emerged. There was no sign of the black horse.

Molly drew in a shuddering breath, torn between horror and absolute delight. Now she understood what Kelvin was. Now his wildness all made perfect, crazy sense.

"Oh, my gosh," she whispered. "He's a kelpie!"

CHAPTER NINE

It was unbelievable, Molly thought, and yet it had to be true. Didn't it?

What else could explain Kelvin's amazing ability to communicate with horses? The way he was able to swim without seeming to get wet? The way he could make the impossible climb to Molly's bedroom window, then vanish without a trace? His incredible knack for inspiring mischief?

Yes, it had to be. But . . .

"What's a kelpie doing on Blackberry Island?" Molly murmured.

Though he was much too far away to have heard her, Kelvin's sleek, dark head suddenly turned toward the trees where Molly was concealed. For a moment she was sure he had seen her, though she knew with the logical part of her mind that it was impossible.

Then he turned away and Molly let out her breath. And suddenly she knew why he was there. The answer was plain.

The Sith-stone!

The black stone must be genuine after all, Molly thought excitedly. Uncle Jack, with his knack for sending unusual gifts, had outdone himself this time, even though he didn't know it. He'd sent her a real magic charm, and now she had power over a water spirit!

"I don't believe this," she mumbled aloud. "I've got to talk to Josh!"

Turning, she began to pick her way back up the slope. Near the top, she remembered that she'd come to warn Kelvin about the sheriff, but she didn't turn back. Kelvin the strange, wild boy she would have worried about. Kelvin the kelpie could take care of himself.

When she got to Josh's house, his mother answered the door. "Oh, hi, Molly," she said. "You just missed Josh. He's on his way to watch a baseball game at the high school. If you go by way of Paul Roman's house, you might catch him."

"Thanks, Ms. Goldberg," Molly said, and ran off. She had to find Josh before he met up with Paul.

Paul lived on East Oak Street, in the newer part of town. Cutting across Founder's Green, she spotted Josh just as he was turning the corner onto Paul's block. "Josh!" she yelled, waving both arms.

He stopped and waited for her to catch up with him. "What's up?" he asked as she puffed to a halt.

"I have to talk to you," she panted. "It's really important."

"Now?" Josh said. "Paul's waiting for me. Um, do you want to come to the game with us?" He looked uncomfortable. Paul sometimes made cracks about Molly being Josh's girlfriend, Molly knew.

She shook her head. "No. Josh, listen! It's about Kelvin. I know what he is."

"*What* he is?" Josh repeated, frowning.

"Yes. Josh, he's not human!" Molly blurted. "He's a kelpie!"

"He's a what?" Josh wrinkled his face.

"A kelpie. It's a kind of water spirit from Scotland. That's why he always has water-weeds in his hair. All kelpies do, that's how you recognize them. And it explains the hoofprints on the shore. And get this—I have a Sith-stone that gives me power over him! That's why he's here!"

Josh was looking worried. "O'Brien, are you feeling all right?" he asked.

Molly stamped her foot. "I'm fine," she said. "Just listen for a minute, will you?"

"Okay, okay," Josh said. "Go ahead."

So Molly explained everything from the beginning: how Uncle Jack had sent her the Sith-stone and the books; how Kelvin had appeared the next day; all that she'd read about kelpies; and how she'd just seen Kelvin apparently transform himself from a horse into a boy.

When she finished talking, Josh stood there in silence for a moment, chewing thoughtfully on his thumbnail. Then he looked up at her. "You know, you could be wrong," he said. "I'm pretty sure I could come up with a logical explanation for everything you just told me. I mean, you didn't actually see him change from a horse into a person, did you?"

Molly just looked at him.

Josh shrugged. "Okay," he said. "So Kelvin is a kelpie. I guess we should come up with a plan to deal with it, huh?"

Molly broke into a wide smile. She had known Josh would take her seriously in the end. Even if she didn't have any proof, he knew she wasn't crazy. That was one of the things that made him the coolest kid she knew.

"Can you get out of going to the game with Paul?" she asked.

"Wait here," Josh said.

Molly watched him run up the street to Paul's house and knock at the door. He was back a few moments later. "Now Paul thinks I'm nuts," he said. "Oh, well."

"Sorry," Molly said sincerely.

They headed down Oak Street toward one of

Molly's favorite talking spots, the bandstand in Founder's Green. As they walked past the tall bronze statue of Jan van Huyten, the island's first settler and founder of the town, Molly reached out and gave it an affectionate pat on the leg. "Good old Jan," she said. "I wish we could go back into the tunnels, don't you?"

"Yeah," Josh agreed.

Beneath the statue ran a whole network of old smugglers' tunnels. The smugglers had even drilled peepholes through Jan Van Huyten's eyes so that you could stand inside the statue and peek out at the town. Molly, Josh, and Gwen had had some amazing adventures in the tunnels, until a section had collapsed one day. After that, all their parents had declared the tunnels off-limits.

"About Kelvin," Josh said. "What are we going to do with him?"

"I'm not sure whether we really have to *do* anything or not," Molly said. She climbed the stairs to the bandstand and sat down on the top step. "I mean, if he's magic he can take care of himself, right?"

"O'Brien," Josh said, leaning against the handrail. "Remember what you said about that stone your uncle sent you?"

"The Sith-stone?" Molly frowned. "What about it?"

Josh spread out his hands. "Don't you get it? If all this stuff is really true, then Kelvin is in your power. You can make him do whatever you want."

"Josh!" Molly stared at him in horror. "You want me to treat him like a slave? Make him fetch and carry and bow to me every time he comes into a room? That's awful!"

"No, no," Josh said impatiently. "Get real, O'Brien. That isn't what I meant at all."

"Well, what did you mean?" Molly demanded.

"Don't think of him as a slave," Josh said. "Think of him as . . . as a genie. You know, like in the *Arabian Nights*. He can bring you cool stuff. He can take you places you could never go on your own."

"Well, I wouldn't make him steal for me," Molly said stoutly. She frowned doubtfully. "I guess he could bring me stuff from the sea. Like lobsters and fish. Big deal."

"And treasure from wrecks," Josh added.

"Oh!" Molly's eyes widened with excitement. "Now I see what you're talking about."

"At last," Josh grumbled. "You're smart, O'Brien, but sometimes you aren't very practical."

"And, Josh," Molly went on, ignoring his comment. Her imagination was starting to work. "I bet he could take us riding on dolphins and whales and stuff. Maybe he could even introduce us to the Loch Ness Monster! Wow, this could be so cool!"

"Right!" Josh said, laughing. He held up his hand and Molly gave him a high-five.

"Hi, you guys," a girl's voice called.

Molly turned around. Ann Chiu was coming toward them across the green.

"Hi!" Molly said. "What are you doing?"

Ann's pretty face was set in a scowl. "Well, I was supposed to be going to the baseball game with Charlotte, but she stood me up," she said.

"You, too?" Molly asked sympathetically. "She did that to me while we were working on our science project."

"This is the third time this week," Ann complained. "She was supposed to come over Thursday night, but she never showed. Then last night my big brother was going to take us to the movies on the mainland, but Charlotte never showed for that, either. And now this!" She shook her head. "I think she's been sneaking off to see some boy she has a crush on, but she won't admit anything."

"Boy?" Molly's attention suddenly perked up. "What boy?"

"I don't know," Ann said. "I think he's older. Charlotte said he was Scottish or something, and had this funny accent."

So Charlotte had been hanging around with Kelvin! Molly shot a quick look at Josh. He was frowning.

Suddenly she thought of something that made all the blood drain from her face. She let out an involuntary gasp, then turned it into a cough as Ann and Josh looked at her.

"Hey, are you guys going to the game?" Ann asked hopefully. "I'll go with you."

"Uh—no, we aren't going," Molly said quickly. "We have to leave now, Ann. We, uh, we promised my dad we'd help him clean out the basement."

"Oh." Ann looked disappointed. "Okay, well, see you later, I guess."

"Bye," Molly and Josh said together.

The minute Ann was out of earshot, Molly was on her feet. "Josh, I think we have a problem," she said.

"I thought we might," Josh said. "Your face just turned the color of cream cheese. What's up?"

"We have to get to my house right away," Molly said. "Let's walk. I'll explain as we go."

They set off. "I'm listening," Josh said.

"Remember yesterday, when I was complaining about Charlotte and I said I wanted to get revenge on her?" Molly said. "And remember how Kelvin said if I wasn't going to do anything to her, he'd do it for me?"

"Yeah, but—" Josh broke off, then let out a whistle. "I get it. You think because you're his master he'll actually do something?"

Molly nodded numbly.

"Hmm." Josh pursed his lips. They went past the gas station at the edge of town. After a moment he said, "Well, maybe you should let him. Someone should teach Charlotte a lesson."

"No. You don't understand," Molly said miserably. "You don't know what kelpies do."

Josh looked faintly annoyed. "Then maybe you should tell me."

Molly gulped. "They lure people into the water. And I think if a kelpie gets you to go into the water with him, then you never come out."

CHAPTER TEN

Josh's head whipped around and he stared at Molly with wide eyes for a second. Then he said, "I think we better run."

"Right," Molly agreed grimly.

The two of them raced up the road. Soon Molly had a stitch in her side, but she pushed on. When they came to Welcome Inn, she turned and started up the driveway.

"No time to stop," Josh panted. "We have to get to DeKater Hollow!"

"Have to get the stone," Molly said. "Might need it . . . to stop him."

Josh nodded and they labored up the hill. Banging open the front door, Molly ran through the hall and up the stairs while Josh collapsed on the porch glider.

Gwen, coming out of her room on the second floor, watched open-mouthed as her sister tore by.

"What's wrong? Do you have to use the bathroom or something?" she called. But Molly didn't stop to answer.

By the time she reached her own room on the third floor, her heart was pumping so hard she thought it might jump right out of her chest. Colored circles swam in front of her eyes and she couldn't seem to get her breath back.

This was ridiculous, she thought. She and Josh would never get to Kelvin in time if they killed themselves running to DeKater Hollow!

Bracing her arms on her desk, she put her head down and waited until her breathing came a little easier. Then she slipped the Sith-stone in her pocket and clattered down the stairs again.

She threw open her sister's door. "I need to borrow your bike," she said without ceremony.

"What's wrong with yours?" Gwen asked.

"Nothing. Josh is going to use it. Please, Gwen, we're in a big hurry."

Gwen's blue eyes narrowed in suspicion. "Why? What are you doing? Is it something fun? Can I come, too?"

"Not if I borrow your bike," Molly pointed out. "Come on, Gwen, please!"

"Are you having an adventure?" Gwen demanded, folding her arms. "That's it, isn't it?

You're having an adventure, and you didn't even tell me. I can't believe it!"

"Gwen!" Molly clenched her teeth. She didn't have time to argue with her sister right now.

But Gwen was pouting. "You always leave me out of *everything*," she said in a hurt voice.

Molly took a deep breath. "Look," she said. "I didn't even know I was having an adventure until about twenty minutes ago, or I would have told you before. And anyway, this adventure is more of a nightmare! You'd hate it, believe me."

"Is it scary?" Gwen's eyes widened.

"Very," Molly said emphatically. "And it's about to get even scarier, unless you let me borrow your bike. I promise I'll tell you all about it later."

Gwen was quiet for a moment more. Then she gave a little nod. "Okay," she muttered.

"Thank you." Turning, Molly flew down the stairs and out to the porch. "Come on," she said to Josh. "Let's ride."

They ran around to the shed by the kitchen and wheeled out the bikes. "I have to ride a girl's bike?" Josh complained. But at the look on Molly's face he caught himself. "Never mind."

With Molly leading the way, they skimmed back down the driveway and along the shortcut to DeKater Hollow.

"Oof," Josh groaned as they bumped over the uneven ground of the overgrown lane. "I hope these bikes are strong. This is a pretty rough road."

"It's about to get worse," Molly told him. "Hold on!"

She steered Gwen's bike off the lane and into the woods. Behind her she could hear Josh muttering under his breath. "What?" she called.

"I was just saying that if we do get there in time to save Charlotte, I might drown her myself for all the trouble she put us through," Josh called back. "Ouch! Oof!"

"Sorry!" Molly yelled.

Then they were swooping down the hill and both of them were working too hard at avoiding the trees to say anything at all.

At the bottom of the hill they barreled out into the meadow with the butternut tree. Josh brought Molly's bike to a skidding stop and jumped off. "Do you see either of them?" he called, looking around.

Molly shaded her eyes with her hands and peered up and down the shoreline. The day was still, with the promise of heat. And as far as she could see, the lake was tranquil and empty. "No," she said with a sinking heart. "Josh, what if we're too late? What will we do?"

"Don't think like that," Josh advised. "Come on, let's look for them."

It was Charlotte's high-pitched giggle that led them to the reedy islets at the far end of the lake. Molly grabbed Josh's arm. "Did you hear that? It was her. I know that giggle!"

"It came from farther up, I think," Josh said, pointing.

They pushed through the reeds, batting at the clouds of gnats that swarmed instantly around their heads. "It's like hacking through a jungle," Josh whispered. "If only we had machetes."

Suddenly Molly heard Charlotte's voice again. This time it was behind them and to the right. At the water's edge, Molly thought with a chill.

"But I don't have a bathing suit," Charlotte was saying.

"That way," Molly hissed, and started blundering toward the sound.

"Och, what do you need one of those things for?" Kelvin's voice replied. "We're only going for a bit of a wade. Come on—take my hand. There. Don't worry, I won't let go of you."

Molly turned pale at his last words.

Molly and Josh burst through onto the lake shore. The reeds here fringed a little half-moon of open ground. Charlotte and Kelvin were standing at the edge of the lake, hands clasped together. The water was almost lapping their toes.

"*Stop!*" Molly yelled.

Charlotte and Kelvin turned around. When Charlotte's eyes fell on Molly, her face twisted into a scowl. "What do *you* want?" she said. "Why don't you stop following Kelvin and get lost?"

Molly set her teeth. "Charlotte, you can't go in the water with Kelvin," she said.

"Says who?" Charlotte demanded.

"*You* can't argue with her. She'll never listen," Josh told Molly in a rapid undertone. "Let me deal with her. You talk to Kelvin."

Stepping forward, he took Charlotte's arm.

"What are you doing?" Charlotte said suspiciously. "Let go of me!"

"I have something very serious to tell you," Josh said gravely. "You'd better come with me."

"But—" Charlotte wailed as he dragged her away. She looked over her shoulder at Kelvin. "Do something!"

Kelvin spread out his hands. "What can I do, now, girl?" he called. His eyes were bright with mischief. "It looks as if the best lad won. I can't fight fate, can I?"

A mortified expression appeared on Josh's face. In the last glimpse Molly had of him before he disappeared with a bewildered Charlotte, the tips of his ears were bright red.

Then Molly swung around to face Kelvin. "Kelvin, you can't do stuff like that! You just can't!" she exclaimed.

"Like what?" he inquired. His face showed only polite puzzlement.

"Oh, don't." Molly stamped her foot. "You can't bluff me anymore. I know what you are, and I know what you were about to do with Charlotte. You were going to drown her!"

"Was I really?" Kelvin looked interested.

"Yes!" Delving into her overalls pocket, Molly brought out the Sith-stone and held it up for him to see. "I figured it all out. I know the stone really works, and that's why you're here. You came during the big storm on Monday night, didn't you? That's why, when I met you, you said that thing about it being a hard journey."

"Did I, now?" Kelvin murmured.

"Yes. I didn't get it then, but after this morning, I do. I saw you go into these reeds right here as a horse and come out as you are now. I guess you didn't tell me because you didn't want me to know you were in my power. But now that I know, you might as well admit you're a kelpie."

"A kelpie?" Kelvin said the word as if he'd never heard it before.

"You know," Molly said. She was starting to get frustrated. "A water spirit."

"That's what you think I am?" His voice was gentle, and his brown eyes full of concern.

Molly gritted her teeth. Josh had said that trying to get a straight answer out of Kelvin was like talking to a brick wall, but she thought it was more like talking to a mirror. All you got back was a reflection of yourself, red-faced and ridiculous and saying crazy things. . . .

No! The things she was saying weren't crazy!

Kelvin was trying to make her doubt the truth.

Suddenly she was angry. "Fine," she said. "You want me to believe you're not a kelpie? Okay. You're not a kelpie. You're just an ordinary kid." She shook the Sith-stone at him. "But from now on you better act like one. Got it?"

The moment the words were out, she caught her breath. She should have thought first, before using the stone to control him. Who knew how it would work? Would there be another thunderstorm? Would lightning come and strike Kelvin down?

But nothing happened. The sun continued to shine and the grasshoppers to drone into the still, shimmering air. It didn't work, Molly thought, alarmed.

Well, she still had to try to make Kelvin understand. "Look," she said. "I guess you thought you were helping me, but please, let me deal with Charlotte on my own, okay? I mean, just because you, uh, work for me, I can't let you go around killing people I don't like. I'll be arrested!"

Just then Josh came back. "She went home," he reported.

Molly let out a sigh of relief. Charlotte was safe—at least for now.

"I told her Kelvin might be a carrier of Scotch plague," Josh went on. "I said it was a disease you could get from Scottish people who lived around lakes."

Molly stared. "She believed that?"

"No, I don't think so," Josh said.

"Then why did she go?" Molly asked, puzzled.

Josh looked glum. "I think she thinks I was trying to get her away from Kelvin because *I* like her," he mumbled. Glaring at Kelvin, he added, "Thanks a lot. Now she'll never leave me alone!"

Relief was making Molly feel giddy. She bit her lip, trying not to laugh. "Wow, Josh, that's awful," she said. Then she couldn't hold it in anymore. A snort escaped her, then a giggle. And then she was cracking up.

Josh switched his glare to her. "It isn't funny," he snapped. "Cut that out, O'Brien!"

"Sorry," Molly said, gasping. "It's just—" She broke off, seized by another fit of laughter.

"I'm going now," Josh said coldly. "Maybe I can catch the rest of the game with Paul. I've had enough of girls for one day."

"Kelvin, I have to go," Molly said breathlessly. She started after Josh. "Wait, Josh, I'll ride back with you. Come on, I said I was sorry. Anyway, I wasn't laughing at you, I was laughing *with* you. Really, Josh!"

Long after their voices faded away, Kelvin stood in the same spot, staring after them. His face was blank and still. In the dark coils of his hair, a tiny fleck of seaweed glistened green.

Then, after a while, the fleck began to turn brown.

CHAPTER ELEVEN

During the following week, Molly and Josh went to DeKater Hollow several times, looking for Kelvin. But they couldn't find any sign of him.

Nor did they hear anything about him. Sheriff Choate had been unable to find him, though he'd been to DeKater Hollow twice looking. And Kelvin's nightly pranks seemed to have stopped completely. It was as if he had vanished from the face of the earth.

By Thursday afternoon, on their third trip to the hollow, Molly began to seriously worry. Could Kelvin have gone back to Scotland? she wondered.

"O'Brien!" Josh hailed her from a rocky patch of ground near a clump of spruce trees.

"Look at this," he said when she came running

up. He pointed at the remains of a fire in a small hollow lined with flat stones. Several charred corncobs had been tossed on the blackened embers.

"Do you think this was Kelvin's fire?" Molly asked.

Josh nodded. "I haven't seen anyone else camping around DeKater Hollow." He stirred the ashes with his foot. "Some of these coals are still warm. I bet Kelvin made the fire this morning to cook his breakfast."

"I guess that means he's still around," Molly said, a little wistfully. After a moment, she asked, "Josh, do you think he's mad at us for taking Charlotte away from him? Do you think that's why we haven't seen him?"

"Maybe," Josh said. "But we couldn't have done anything else. You know that."

"I know," Molly agreed. She still felt sad, though. It was hard to think of Kelvin as bad, somehow. He was what he was, and he couldn't help it any more than a tornado could help being a tornado.

"Anyway, I bet it would make him feel better to know how much I'm suffering for what we did," Josh added gloomily. "Charlotte hasn't stopped making googly-eyes at me all week."

Molly smiled absently, staring at the corncobs in the fireplace. "You know, I never thought of Kelvin as someone who needed to eat," she said after a moment.

"I guess kelpies have to eat like everyone else," Josh said. "I wonder where he got the food, though."

He probably stole it from some farmer, Molly reflected. She doubted that kelpies carried money with them.

She sighed. "I hope he's okay," she said. "I feel kind of responsible for him, you know?"

"O'Brien, he's a kelpie," Josh pointed out. "He's magic. He's probably even . . . what-do-you-call-it . . . immortal. How could he not be okay? Stop worrying."

"I'll try," Molly said.

But somehow, she couldn't manage to do it.

On Saturday evening, the Blackberry Island Nature Society held its annual picnic at DeKater Hollow. Molly's whole family went. Though Mrs. O'Brien had protested, for once Mr. O'Brien had put his foot down and the dining room at Welcome Inn was closed for the evening.

During the first couple of hours of the picnic, Molly kept a sharp eye out for Kelvin, half in hope and half in worry. She would have liked to see him and find out what he'd been doing all week, but at the same time she knew that it would be risky for him to make an appearance. Though the uproar over the speedboats had died down, it would flare up again if the sheriff thought Kelvin was still on the island.

But as the evening shadows lengthened and

there was no sign of him, Molly began to think Kelvin would stay hidden. "I guess he figured out that people would be mad at him about the boats," she said to Josh as they stuffed themselves with barbecued chicken and potato salad.

Josh put down his gnawed drumstick and licked his fingers. "Maybe he finally got some common sense," he suggested. "Oh, man, that was my fifth piece of chicken. I think my stomach might burst."

"That's gross," Molly remarked. Leaning back against a big, sun-warmed rock, she stretched out her legs and gave a contented sigh. "But I know what you mean."

All around them was the happy din of a hundred other picnickers at the end of a long, sun-filled day. In the butternut field, Andrew O'Brien and a bunch of other boys were playing Ultimate Frisbee. On the lake, several canoes full of kids and teenagers paddled about. Molly watched them idly, squinting against the late sun. Slowly, her eyes drifted shut.

"Hey, you guys."

Molly opened her eyes. Gwen was standing over her. "What?" she asked lazily.

Gwen dropped down beside Molly. "That magic boy, Kelvin," she began.

"What about him?" Josh asked. Gwen knew the whole story of Kelvin by now. As promised, Molly had told her all about it after they rescued Charlotte the weekend before.

"Does he wear a red vest?" Gwen asked.

"Yes, why?" Molly sat up, suddenly alert.

"I just saw him," Gwen announced. "He was trying to snag a hot dog off the Andersons' barbecue while no one was there. Then Mrs. Anderson came back and screamed when she saw him, and he ran away."

"Oh, no!" Molly scrambled to her feet. "Did anyone go after him?"

Gwen nodded. "Mr. Anderson and a couple of other men."

"Josh, what should we do?" Molly asked, her eyes wide with worry.

Josh stood up, too, and pushed his hair out of his face. "There's nothing we can do," he said. "Either they'll catch him or they won't. We can't stop them. But I bet they won't. Remember how sure he was that he wouldn't get caught that night at the Hunt Club? And he was right."

"Yeah, but . . ." Molly trailed off, gnawing on her thumb. Josh had a good point. Still, she couldn't shake the anxiety that had been dogging her ever since they'd last seen Kelvin.

"I guess you're right," she said at last. Just then a Frisbee came swooping toward them. "Heads up, Josh!" yelled Paul Roman.

Launching himself into the air, Josh grabbed the Frisbee and sent it soaring back. "I'm going to get in on this game. Just chill out," he advised Molly.

"Everything will be fine."

Nodding, Molly stuffed her hands into her pockets and tried to watch the game.

Twenty minutes later, Gwen nudged Molly's elbow. "There's Mr. Anderson," she whispered. "He's back!"

Molly spun around. Charlotte's father, a big, heavyset man with fading fair hair and prominent eyes, was stamping toward his wife. He was red-faced and irritable. Behind him were two other men Molly recognized from town.

"It looks like they lost him," Molly said, feeling a surge of relief. "Let's go see if we can find out what happened." With Gwen beside her, she set out at a fast walk over to the Andersons' picnic blanket, near the edge of the woods.

Mr. Anderson's voice rose in anger just as the two girls drew near. "I can't help it if the little hooligan got away," he snapped.

"We almost had him," one of the other men volunteered. "Chased him right down to the edge of the lake. But then he doubled back. Slipped right in between me and George, Mrs. Anderson. After that we lost him in the woods."

Molly frowned. "He was right at the lake's edge! Why didn't he hide in the water?" she whispered to Gwen.

"Huh?" Gwen said. "How could he do that?"

"He's a kelpie. A water spirit. The lake is like his

home," Molly explained. Her frown deepened. "I don't get it."

Gwen waved a hand. "Shh. I want to hear."

"Mother always said you were lazy, Stanley, but I never believed her until now," Mrs. Anderson was saying. "You couldn't even catch one boy!"

"For Pete's sake, Evelyn, he ran like a deer! Would you stop nagging me?"

"Nagging?" Mrs. Anderson said sharply. "Well, I like that. It may not matter to you that the boy nearly cost us several thousand dollars on our boat, Stanley—"

"We got the boat back, didn't we?" Mr. Anderson muttered. "Let the sheriff take care of the kid. *If* the kid's the one who did it."

"But it matters to me," Mrs. Anderson swept on, ignoring the interruption. "Now, I want you to get some men together, go back out there, and find that boy!"

"Give it a rest, Evelyn," Mr. Anderson said, and turned away. Catching sight of Molly and Gwen, he scowled. "What do you kids want?"

"Nothing," Molly said quickly. "Excuse us."

Taking Gwen by the arm, she pulled her away.

"Wow," Gwen said in an undertone. "What an awful family!"

"Aren't they?" Molly agreed. "Look, Gwen, there's something weird going on with Kelvin. He's not acting normal."

"How do you know what's normal for a kelpie?" Gwen asked.

"Okay, maybe I don't," Molly said irritably. "But I think I know Kelvin, at least a little. I mean, to start with, stealing hot dogs just doesn't seem like his style."

"Okay. What should we do?" Gwen asked.

By now they were walking past a row of canoes that were drawn up on the beach. A light wind had kicked up, making wavelets on the lake. Molly turned and looked at the group of boys playing Frisbee. The sun was almost below the horizon, and people were starting to leave the picnic, but the game showed no signs of slowing down.

"We should talk to Josh," she began, "but—"

She broke off and whirled around as someone started screaming behind her.

"Look! Out on the lake!" a woman yelled, pointing. "That canoe is sinking. Someone help those two girls! They'll never make it to shore!"

Molly gasped at the sight of the two small figures flailing around by an overturned canoe. They were way out in the middle of the lake!

Everyone at the picnic ran toward the shore. A muscular boy of about eighteen led the way, stopping at the water's edge to peer out for a second. Molly recognized him as Ann Chiu's older brother, Tony.

"Oh, no," he said. "That's my sister!"

"And that's my daughter with her," said a man's voice. Turning, Molly saw Stanley Anderson, his normally ruddy face pale. "Charlotte's not a strong swimmer."

"Neither is Ann," Tony said.

Molly gasped. Ann and Charlotte were drowning!

CHAPTER TWELVE

In the next instant, Tony Chiu kicked off his shoes, grabbed an orange flotation cushion from a nearby canoe, and bounded through the water. Two of his friends dashed in after him.

Grandpa Lloyd shouldered his way to the front of the crowd. "Hang on to the paddles, girls!" he boomed, cupping his hands around his mouth. "Hang on, and don't panic! Help is on the way!"

Molly found herself clasping her hands tightly together as she watched the three young men swim toward the girls.

"Tony used to work summers as a lifeguard at Chapin Bay Beach," Josh said, coming up beside her. "So did one of those other guys. Ann and Charlotte will be okay."

Indeed, a moment later Tony reached his sister. Straining to see through the gathering darkness, Molly watched the two dark heads as they began to move slowly toward shore.

"I think Darryl's got Charlotte," Josh reported. "Yeah, they're coming in."

Molly sagged with relief.

"Look, the canoe's sinking," Gwen said. "It must have been swamped by a wave."

"I doubt if that was it," Molly said. She spoke softly, not wanting any of the grown-ups who were standing around to overhear. "Last time I was in a canoe with Charlotte, the same thing nearly happened to us. She was messing around, trying to stand up and stuff. I think Kelvin used some magic to stop us from going over."

"Funny to think of a kelpie trying to stop you from drowning," Josh commented.

"You don't think . . ." Gwen began, then hesitated. "You don't think what just happened was Kelvin's fault? I mean, since you stopped him last time he tried to get Charlotte."

"No way," Molly said. "That isn't how kelpies do it. They lure you into the water; they don't tip over your boat once you're already there."

Gwen looked relieved. "Oh, good."

"Here they come," Josh said. "Now we'll hear what really happened."

The two girls stumbled out of the lake,

supported by their rescuers, and were immediately surrounded by their concerned families.

"Oh, you poor lambs! Come sit over here," Ann's mother said, guiding them to stools around one of the barbecue grills that were still going. "Someone get a couple of blankets, quickly!"

"Isn't there a doctor here?" Charlotte's mother demanded. "Stanley, go get my cellular phone from the car. We'll call an ambulance."

"No! We're okay, really," Ann said. She was shivering and her voice trembled, but Molly suspected she was more frightened and embarrassed than anything else.

The blankets were brought and wrapped around Ann and Charlotte's shoulders. "Now, tell us what happened," Ann's mother said.

"First of all, how come you were out in a canoe without life jackets or flotation cushions?" Tony broke in.

"If there weren't any in the canoe," Mrs. Anderson said, "I'll sue whoever owns it for negligence."

Molly rolled her eyes. "Oh, please," she muttered.

There was a long silence. Then Ann spoke up.

"There were life jackets," she admitted. "We took them out. We thought we wouldn't need them." She darted a look at Charlotte.

"I can guess whose idea that was," Josh whispered. "Charlotte looks like she wants to kill Ann for telling."

Tony seemed angry. "Ann, you know better than that."

"But how did you tip over?" Mr. Anderson asked. "There wasn't that much wind."

Both girls were silent again. Ann was very unhappy. Charlotte's face, lit by the glow of the charcoal, was sullen.

"Well?" Ann's father prodded. "You weren't horsing around in the canoe, were you?"

Ann appeared to be even more unhappy.

"No, we weren't," Charlotte said, but she wouldn't look up. "It wasn't our fault. There was—there was a hole in the canoe!"

"A hole!" Molly exclaimed. She saw the look of blank surprise on Ann's face.

"No!" Mrs. Anderson gasped, looking shocked and outraged.

"I didn't see any hole," Ann said.

Charlotte licked her lips. "Ann couldn't see it. It was right under my seat."

Everyone in the crowd was murmuring, looking at one another. A lot of people seemed skeptical, Molly noticed.

"She's lying," Josh whispered with certainty. "She doesn't want to admit it was her fault."

"Charlotte, are you sure?" Mrs. Chiu asked.

"I'd like to see that hole," someone else said.

"That'll be hard," Grandpa Lloyd observed. "The canoe's at the bottom of the lake."

Mrs. Anderson turned an outraged glare on him. "My Charlotte is not a liar," she snapped. "Of course there was a hole. And what's more, I think we all know exactly how it got there!"

Everyone murmured some more. "Excuse me," Mr. O'Brien said. "I'm afraid I don't follow you."

"It's obvious," Mrs. Anderson said. "For two weeks now, we've been vandalized and terrorized by this young hoodlum, this wild boy in a red vest who camps in the woods."

Molly felt a cold fist close around her heart. Kelvin!

Mrs. Anderson's voice grew shriller and angrier. "And now this. He *deliberately* knocks a hole in a canoe, just for kicks, not caring about the people that might get hurt because of him. Well, it's time we dealt with him. Now. Tonight. He should be put away. He's a menace!"

There was a shocked silence. Even Charlotte looked taken aback. Staring at her mother, she opened her mouth as if to say something. But then she shut it again.

Molly, watching her, nudged Josh. "Make Charlotte say whether or not it's true," she whispered urgently. "I bet even she won't have the gall to say Kelvin did it."

Josh's eyes narrowed. "Charlotte, did you see Ke—uh, this boy near the canoes?" he called.

Charlotte flushed and looked down. "I didn't see

anyone," she muttered. "All I know is, there was a hole in the stupid canoe."

"Just because my daughter didn't see him doesn't mean he wasn't there," Mrs. Anderson snapped. "We know he was lurking around here earlier. I saw him try to steal a hot dog off my own grill!"

"But you didn't see him knock a hole in a canoe," Grandpa Lloyd reminded her in a dry voice.

Mrs. Anderson's lips twisted. "Don't you think he knows how not to be seen? We're talking about a devious criminal here!"

"Oh, for the love of Mike," Grandpa Lloyd burst out, disgusted. "Devious criminal? From the descriptions I've heard, the boy can't be more than fifteen years old!"

"My father's right," Mrs. O'Brien chimed in. Her blue eyes blazed with indignation. "I can't believe we're all standing here like this discussing a—a witch hunt! For a mere child!"

"You tell them, Mom!" Molly cheered.

"No!" a man said from near the back of the crowd. "I'm with Evelyn Anderson. I say we find him. That 'mere child' cost me my brand-new boat."

"Good riddance. It was a noisy stinkpot!" someone else yelled. Then everyone was shouting again.

"People!" Mr. LaGamba, the vice-principal, called, holding up both hands. "Please!"

When the crowd hushed he turned to Mrs.

O'Brien and Grandpa Lloyd. "I appreciate your feelings of sympathy for the boy," he said. "But I must emphasize that this is not a witch hunt."

"It isn't?" Mrs. O'Brien said. "Then what do you call it when a bunch of adults are planning to sweep the area at night, hunting for a defenseless boy, without even trying to contact the sheriff or any other legitimate authorities?"

"There isn't time to call in the sheriff," Mr. LaGamba replied with exaggerated patience. "But, good heavens, Mrs. O'Brien, we're not savages! We aren't going to lynch the boy, or beat him. Obviously he's a very troubled youth. He needs help. He needs discipline. And you have my word that he will receive it. We'll turn him over to the juvenile authorities and *they* will judge his case and decide the appropriate punishment."

"You can be his lawyer, if you're so worried about him," Mrs. Anderson said to Mrs. O'Brien.

"If he needs me, I will," Mrs. O'Brien retorted. Under her breath, she added, "Repulsive woman!"

"Anyone who wants to help search, come over here by the big tree," Mr. LaGamba called.

Molly was glad to see that only about fifteen people responded. "I bet they're all speedboat owners," Gwen whispered.

Mr. LaGamba began organizing the searchers into teams. "George, Victor, Ted, Bob, you go with Stan Anderson and comb the woods on the east and south shores of the lake. Have you got flashlights with you? Good. I'll take a team through the west and north woods. Who'll come with me?"

In the hum of activity, Charlotte and Ann sat forgotten on their stools. Josh stepped up to Charlotte. "Nice going," he growled. "Once again you blame somebody else for something that's your fault. You're unbelievable."

"Yeah," Ann chimed in. She stood up, her pretty face angry. "I can't believe you, Charlotte. You know as well as I do that there was no hole in the canoe. It tipped over because we were messing around. Why did you have to lie about it? Now they're blaming someone who had nothing to do with it."

"There *was* a hole," Charlotte insisted in a sullen voice.

Ann shook her head. "I don't think I want to be friends with you anymore," she said, and walked away.

Charlotte flushed a deep red. Molly saw tears well up in her eyes. As she huddled on her stool, wrapped in her blanket with her hair in a sodden mass, she suddenly looked lonely and pathetic.

But Molly couldn't summon up much sympathy. For one thing, there wasn't time. Grabbing Josh and Gwen by the arm, she dragged them off into the darkness.

"This is awful," she said as soon as they were out of earshot of the crowd. "They're going to send

Kelvin to reform school, or a foster home, or some-thing even worse, even though we *know* he didn't put a hole in that canoe. We have to help him!"

"I agree it's awful," Josh said. "Charlotte's mother is ten times worse than Charlotte. But, O'Brien, I keep telling you Kelvin won't get caught! He can take care of himself."

"No, he can't," Molly said flatly. "At least, I don't think he can. Gwen and I were just coming to talk to you about it when the canoe accident happened. There's something wrong with Kelvin."

Quickly, with Gwen chiming in, she told Josh how Kelvin had run into the woods instead of the water when the men were chasing him.

"That *is* weird," Josh admitted when she was done. "Do you think he's sick or something?"

"I don't know," Molly said. "All I know is, we have to find him before the grown-ups do."

Gwen grabbed Molly's and Josh's arms and pulled them into a huddle. "So how do we do that?" she said. "What's the plan?"

"The plan is, you stay here," Molly began. She held up a hand to stop Gwen from protesting. "Gwen, please. We need you to cover for us in case Mom and Dad start asking where we are. You're a good actress. You can keep them from wondering."

Gwen shut her mouth. In the dark it was hard to tell, but Molly thought she looked faintly pleased. "Oh, all right," she said after a moment.

"Josh, we need a flashlight," Molly said.

"There's one in my mom's car," Josh said. "Come on."

Moving casually, Josh and Molly worked their way back to the parking area and grabbed the flashlight from the glove compartment. Then they were off, creeping cautiously through the treeline. "We'll keep the light off until we get away," Josh said. "There's enough moon so we won't fall flat on our faces, and we don't want anyone to know we're out here."

They decided to start their search in the marshy area at the south end of the lake. It was the place where they had found Kelvin most often, and Molly thought he might have gone back there to hide after being chased by Mr. Anderson.

When they were halfway there, a line of bobbing lights warned them that Mr. Anderson and his search party were heading their way. "Lie flat," Josh hissed, burrowing into the undergrowth. "Keep your face hidden."

Molly did as he told her, pinching her nose as dead leaves threatened to make her sneeze. The night air was cool; she was glad she'd worn long pants that day. She wished she'd thought to bring a sweatshirt, too, like Josh.

The search party tramped by. "Keep it down, boys," Molly heard Mr. Anderson say in a low voice. "He's slippery. We want to surprise him."

A minute later Josh sat up. "One good thing," he

whispered. "They make so much noise trying to keep quiet that they couldn't surprise anyone."

"Let's go," Molly said anxiously.

Five minutes later they were at the edge of the tall reeds. "I think we can turn the light on now," Josh said. "No one will see it in here."

He held the light while Molly walked ahead of him, pushing aside reeds. "Kelvin?" she called softly. "It's us, Molly and Josh. Where are you?"

"O'Brien," Josh said suddenly. He flicked the cone of light to the left. It fell on a figure with dark hair, curled up among the reeds with its arms hugging its knees.

"Kelvin," she said, feeling a rush of relief.

Then he looked up, and Molly suppressed a gasp.

His face was streaked with dirt, and he had dark circles under his eyes. His hair, which Molly had always seen glimmering with beads of moisture, was dry and dusty-looking, flecked with bits of leaf. His white shirt, always so snowy and crisp, was now filthy and wrinkled, with a long tear down one sleeve.

"What happened to you?" Molly demanded. "Are you hurt? Are you sick?"

"There are people out hunting for you. Why aren't you hiding in the water?" Josh chimed in.

"In the water?" Kelvin echoed. A violent shiver shook his whole body. "It's so cold in there. I'd catch my death."

"But . . . the water's your home. You're a kelpie!" Molly exclaimed. She wanted to shake him. What was wrong with him? Why did he look so strange and confused?

Kelvin gave her the ghost of his old smile. "A kelpie, is it?" he said. "But I'm not, you know. I'm just an ordinary kid."

An ordinary kid. The words clanged in Molly's mind. "You mean . . ." she whispered.

"What are you talking about?" Josh exclaimed. Worry made him sound angry. "You're about as ordinary as a person with two heads."

"No, Josh, I know what he means." Molly took a deep breath. Her head was spinning.

"The black stone worked, didn't it?" she said to Kelvin. "When I got mad and told you that if you wanted me to think you were an ordinary kid, you had to act like one, you had to obey me. Right?"

Kelvin just looked at her with dull eyes.

Molly knelt by him. Tears pricked her eyelids. "It's true, isn't it?" she whispered. "You aren't a kelpie anymore!"

CHAPTER THIRTEEN

Kelvin was silent.

"Oh, man," Josh said. He started to pace back and forth. "O'Brien, this is worse than terrible! What are we going to do?"

"I don't know," Molly said miserably. She had a tight feeling in her throat. *Think!* she urged herself.

And then, suddenly, she had an idea. "No, I do know," she said, springing to her feet. "We have to go get the stone and release Kelvin from the spell!"

"You mean, go back to Welcome Inn?" Josh asked. He sucked in his cheeks. "It isn't going to be easy getting out of DeKater Hollow. The woods are full of searchers."

"It's Kelvin's only chance," Molly said. Turning to Kelvin, she held out her hand. "Come on."

"I can't," Kelvin whimpered. "I'm cold. I'm tired. I've blisters from these boots. And I've eaten nothing but corn on the cob for six days."

Molly gave Josh an appalled look. Kelvin was falling apart!

She took a deep breath. "You have to," she told him. "Otherwise they'll put you in a reform school. And, believe me, you'd hate that even more than eating corn on the cob for six days straight. Now, come on. Josh, help me!"

Together they pulled Kelvin to his feet. "I'll go first," Josh told Molly. "You follow Kelvin and make sure he doesn't wander off and get lost."

"Okay," Molly agreed.

She watched as Josh cautiously picked a way through to the edge of the reeds and stuck his head out. "The coast is clear," he whispered a moment later. "Let's go!"

To a symphony of crickets and frogs, the three of them scurried across the open ground between the trees and the forest. Or rather, they tried to scurry. But Kelvin, hobbling along in his riding boots, was painfully slow.

"You can do it. Just keep going," Molly told him in what she hoped was an encouraging voice. It was hard not to sound like a frog herself, though, when her heart was in her throat.

She glanced up at the moon. Does it have to shine quite so brightly? she thought. Kelvin's shirt, even filthy as it was, was very visible.

They were almost to the forest when Kelvin suddenly tripped over a boulder. He pitched to the ground, letting out a cry of pain.

"Get up! Get up! They might have heard you!" Josh whispered frantically. He grabbed Kelvin's arm. "Let's move!"

Someone shouted, faint but clear, behind them. "There he is!"

"Run!" Molly said.

She took one of Kelvin's hands and Josh grabbed the other. Half dragging him with them, they struggled into the shadow of the trees.

"This way," Molly said grimly. She tugged on Kelvin's hand, leading him south. Obediently, he stumbled after her.

"That's the wrong way," Josh said. "Your house is the other direction."

"I know, but they saw us heading that way," Molly explained. "Maybe we can fool them by going this way."

But only a few moments later, she pulled up short at the sight of a line of lights bobbing toward her. "Oh, no," she moaned, horrified. "I led us right into the search party!"

"It was a good idea, anyway," Josh whispered. "Come on, they haven't seen us yet. Hurry!"

Soon, though, it was clear that Kelvin couldn't keep running. "We have to let him rest," Molly told

Josh. "I think he's about to faint or something."

They were on a steep hill now, pocked with tall outcrops of granite. "Over here," Josh said, beckoning them behind one of the big rocks.

Molly led Kelvin over and he sank back against the rock, his chest heaving. His eyes darted from Molly's face to Josh's. "I'm frightened," he said. "Don't let them get me. I couldn't bear it."

Molly gulped. A hopeless feeling threatened to overwhelm her. Blinking back tears, she looked at Josh.

He was pulling his dark hooded sweatshirt over his head. Underneath, she saw, he had on a white T-shirt. "Here," he said, handing the sweatshirt to Kelvin. "Put this on. And give me your vest."

"What are you doing?" Molly demanded.

"He's cold," Josh said. "And he also sticks out in that outfit."

"So that's why you're putting it on?" Molly was outraged. "Do you think you *won't* stick out?"

"Nope," Josh said. "But at least I can outrun a bunch of old guys. I'll catch up with you later, O'Brien. Kelvin, if I don't see you again"—he held up his hand for a high-five—"good luck and all that stuff."

Kelvin stared in bafflement at Josh's hand. After a second Josh lowered it.

"Yeah, whatever," he said, with a lopsided grin. Then he slipped out from behind the rock.

"Josh!" Molly hissed. "Wait! You can't do this. What if they *do* catch you?"

His voice floated back to her. "They won't."

A moment later: "I see him!" a man's voice shouted. "Right there, dead ahead!"

"Hey, kid, stop!" someone else shouted. "We don't want to hurt you."

"He's running away," the first voice said. "Let's get him!"

Heavy footsteps thudded past the rock where Molly and Kelvin were hiding. Molly pressed herself flat, wishing she could melt into the granite and become invisible.

"That way," someone yelled. "The little creep is trying to double back on us!"

Josh was leading them south, Molly guessed. Away from Welcome Inn.

She pushed herself upright. "Let's go," she said to Kelvin. "Josh just gave us the best chance we're going to get."

"You wait here," Molly said, pushing Kelvin down into the shadows by the shed. "Don't move. I'll be right back."

They had made it back to Welcome Inn without further incident, thanks to Josh. And Molly was relieved to discover she had also beaten her family home. That meant there would be no awkward questions to answer.

She hurried around to the back door and unlocked it. Then she raced through the kitchen and up the back stairs to her room. Flipping on the light, she made for her desk and grabbed the Sith-stone. "Gotcha," she said aloud.

Just then she heard a car coming up the hill. Glancing out her window, she recognized Grandpa Lloyd's pickup truck, with her parents jammed into the cab while Andrew and Gwen rode in the back.

"Uh-oh," she muttered, backing away from the window. She slid out of the room and fled down the stairs to the kitchen. It was too late to turn her light off; they'd notice. She'd just have to hope everyone thought she'd left it on earlier.

The back door creaked when you opened it, so Molly timed that with the sounds of the truck's doors opening and shutting. Then, grasping the Sith-stone tightly, she slipped around to where Kelvin was waiting.

"Who's there?" he whispered. "Is it the men chasing me?"

"No, just my family," Molly assured him. "Come on, we're almost there."

Tugging him over the quiet lawn, she ran for the wooden staircase that led down to the ocean beach. The sound of the surf filled her ears as they descended. Finally they were running across the beach to where saltwater hissed silver over the sand. Molly didn't stop until the waves were frothing at their knees.

"The sea is so cold," Kelvin moaned. "It hurts!"

"Not for much longer," Molly promised. She held the Sith-stone up in front of her. "By the power of this stone," she called, "I set you free, Kelvin the Kelpie!"

Then she drew back her arm and threw the black stone out as far as she could. Over and over it turned, catching the moonlight, until finally it vanished into the sea.

A wave crashed in front of them, sending a fountain of salty spray up to drench them both. "Ugh!" Molly exclaimed, spitting out seawater.

When she looked at Kelvin she saw that his black hair was beaded with moisture. A piece of green seaweed was draped over one of his ears and his eyes were bright in the moonlight.

It's from the wave hitting him, she thought, trying to be logical. But . . .

"You're you again!" she said happily.

"Was I ever anyone else?" Kelvin asked.

Molly laughed. "Hey, you answered a question with another question. Now I know you're okay."

There was a short silence. Suddenly Molly felt awkward and strange. "Well, I guess you better get going," she said, looking at the water swishing around her feet. "I mean, I'm sure you're in a hurry to get back to Scotland and see all the other kelpies and stuff, right?"

Kelvin reached out and grasped her hand. "Will

you come for a swim with me?" he asked.

Molly's heart thudded. Her knees felt like jelly. "A . . . a swim?" she quavered.

"Och, don't be afraid. I would never hurt you," Kelvin said. His smile glittered in the moonlight. "We're friends, don't you know?"

As Molly stared at him, the drumming of her pulse in her ears began to block out all other sound, even the booming of the waves. She drew in a deep breath. For some reason, she was feeling dizzy all of a sudden. It was hard to think straight. But in the water, everything would be so much clearer. . . .

"Okay," she whispered, and stepped forward.

"O'Brien!" a cry rang out behind her.

Startled, Molly let go of Kelvin's hand and turned around. Josh was tearing across the beach, a look of horror on his face. A wave slammed into Molly's back and sent her stumbling toward him.

And suddenly she could breathe again. "Holy cow," she said, aghast. "What am I doing?"

"O'Brien, what are you doing?" Josh echoed a second later. "Are you nuts?"

"I . . . I don't know," Molly said. She turned around again. "Kelvin—"

She broke off, her mouth still open. There was no one there!

"What happened?" she gasped. "Where'd he go?"

"He probably knows I was about to pound him,"

Josh said angrily. "Wait till I catch him. I can't believe he was trying to lure you into the water, after all we did for him! What a creep! What a—"

"Listen!" Molly held up her hand.

"What? I don't hear anything," Josh whispered.

Molly had a strange, solemn feeling. "I thought I heard hoofbeats," she said. "I think he's gone."

"Good riddance," Josh pronounced.

Molly wasn't sure if she felt the same way. Kelvin was what he was, and he couldn't help it. Besides . . .

"He said he wouldn't hurt me," she said. "He never lied to us, you know."

"Yeah, well, no offense, but he also had a pretty funny way of telling the truth," Josh pointed out. "Who knows what he *really* meant?"

"I guess you're right. Better not to find out, huh?" Molly swallowed hard. "Thanks, Josh. You might have saved my life."

"Sheesh, O'Brien, forget it," Josh muttered. Molly thought his ears were red, but it was hard to tell in the dim light.

For the first time she noticed that he was no longer wearing Kelvin's red vest. "What'd you do with the vest?" she asked.

Josh grinned suddenly. "Stuck it in the Andersons' picnic basket," he told her.

"That's perfect," Molly said, laughing. "They'll be wondering how it got there for the rest of their lives."

"Yeah," Josh said. He shook his head. "It's been one wild night, O'Brien."

"I know," Molly agreed.

They were both quiet for a while.

"He never admitted it, did he?" Josh asked at last.

"That he was a kelpie? No." Molly shrugged. "It's true, what you said before. There probably is a logical way to explain everything that happened while he was here. And when you come right down to it, we never actually *saw* him do anything magical."

"But we know the truth," Josh said softly.

Molly gazed out at the ocean. Was that a dark head cresting the waves to the east, or was it just a trick of the moon?

"Yes," she said. "We know."

WELCOME INN

Secret in the Moonlight
0-8167-3427-5 $2.95

Ghost of a Chance
0-8167-3428-3 $2.95

The Skeleton Key
0-8167-3429-1 $2.95

The Spell of the Black Stone
0-8167-3579-4 $2.95

Available wherever you buy books.

FOREVER ANGELS

Everyone needs a special angel

Katie's Angel
by Suzanne Weyn

Katie thought she was all alone in the world . . .

When her parents died, Katie's world turned upside down. Forced to move in with uncaring relatives, she's never felt more alone. Katie can't stop missing her parents, and it seems she's always getting into trouble for one reason or another. Finally she can't take it any longer and decides to run away. And that's when Katie discovers that she's not as alone as she thinks she is. There's someone special looking out for her—someone she never would have guessed—who can help Katie find the happiness she's been missing.

0-8167-3614-6 $3.25

Rainbow Bridge®

Available wherever you buy books.

Who is . . .
The Boy on a Black Horse

by Nancy Springer

Gray is intrigued by the new boy in school, the mysterious rider of a magnificent black stallion. The boy, Chav, claims he is a Gypsy prince who, with his younger brother and sister, is searching for his father. Gray herself is still reeling from the loss of her entire family in a tragic accident. She wants to help, but Chav doesn't make it easy. And the more Gray manages to find out, the closer she gets to a horrifying truth that lies at the core of Chav's flight.

Coming in April 1995

0-8167-3633-2 $3.95

Troll Medallion